Scoundrels Shouldn't Be So Charming. . . .

The great Simon Cranston is making coffee for me, Tillie thought with a dazed smile. "I've never had coffee made for me by a celebrity before," she told him as he appeared beside her.

"Have you ever been kissed by a celebrity?" he asked, drawing her into his arms.

"Never."

"Fasten your safety belt," he warned.

His hot lips ignited a raging fever that made her forget her good intentions. Everything else seemed irrelevant to the rising tide of emotions.

"Simon, Simon," she heard someone say in a breathless, longing voice. Her voice!

JOAN SMITH

has written many Regency romances, but likes working with the greater freedom of contemporaries. She also enjoys mysteries and Gothics, collects Japanese porcelain and is a passionate gardener. A native of Canada, she is the mother of three.

Dear Reader:

I'd like to take this opportunity to thank you for all your support and encouragement of Silhouette Romances.

Many of you write in regularly, telling us what you like best about Silhouette, which authors are your favorites. This is a tremendous help to us as we strive to publish the best contemporary romances possible.

All the romances from Silhouette Books are for you, so enjoy this book and the many stories to come. I hope you'll continue to share your thoughts with us, and invite you to write to us at the address below:

Karen Solem
Editor-in-Chief
Silhouette Books
P.O. Box 769
New York, N.Y. 10019

JOAN SMITH
Next Year's Blonde

Silhouette *Romance*

Published by Silhouette Books New York

America's Publisher of Contemporary Romance

SILHOUETTE BOOKS, a Division of Simon & Schuster, Inc.
1230 Avenue of the Americas, New York, N.Y. 10020

Copyright © 1983 by Joan Smith

Distributed by Pocket Books

ISBN: 0-671-57234-2

First Silhouette Books printing July, 1983

10 9 8 7 6 5 4 3 2 1

Map by Ray Lundgren

SILHOUETTE, SILHOUETTE ROMANCE and colophon are
registered trademarks of Simon & Schuster, Inc.

America's Publisher of Contemporary Romance

Printed in the U.S.A.

For my friend
Neff Rotter

Next Year's Blonde

ENGLAND AND SCOTLAND

Places in _italics_ are fictitious.

SCOTLAND

NORTH SEA

IRISH SEA

ENGLAND

WALES

London ★

Maidstone

Chichester

Lyme Regis

Brighton

Wespark

ENGLISH CHANNEL

Chapter One

"You'll never guess who's here!" Gus exclaimed, bursting into his star's dressing room without thinking to knock.

The show's leading lady, Jessica Miter, lifted a well-manicured brow, tossed her mane of blond hair over her shoulder and said, "If you were hoping for a glimpse of something you shouldn't see, Gus darling, you're too late. I've already changed. I have a very important date. I wouldn't want to keep the honorable member waiting, now would I?"

With a wiggle of her shapely hips, she strode past him, leaving a cloud of heavy scent in her wake.

"Who is it, Gus?" Tillie Brennan asked.

Tillie was only the second female lead in the play, chosen by Gus Brooks as much for the physical contrast she presented his star as for her histrionic ability, though she was coming along as an actress.

9

Tillie was dark-haired and fine-boned—what Gus instinctively called a lady, as opposed to the word *dame* that struck him as suitable for Jessica.

"It's Simon Cranston!" Gus said with a wide smile of surprised happiness lighting his face.

"Simon Cranston from London? The BBC Simon Cranston?" Tillie asked, her large gray eyes blinking. "The guy who writes those columns for the newspaper?"

"The one and only Simon Cranston, of 'Simon Says' fame," he confirmed, then added: "That's what he calls his column."

"You'd better stop Jessie. She'll have a fit if she finds out she's missed him. Did he come down to interview her?"

"He's never heard of her. He came to talk to *me*, but he wants to tape an interview for tomorrow's show, and suggested I have some pretty props on hand to decorate the set."

Tillie would normally have been annoyed at this chauvinistic speech. On this occasion, though, she was too happy at the news to be angry. It was a wonderful break for Gus. He had worked hard and invested his life's savings to open his drama workshop. On his parents' deaths, he had inherited a somewhat dilapidated mansion just east of Brighton, on the south coast of England. It had proved his salvation.

Gus had once enjoyed a good reputation in London's West End theater as a bright writer and director of light comedy. After his wife's death some years before, he had, as he inelegantly described it, "gone to the dogs." It would have been more precise to say he had taken to drink. A director who went on three-day binges was not popular, no matter how great his talent. After a tough crawl from the gutter, he pulled himself together, established Brooks' Dramatic

Workshop at his home and began a talent hunt. He collected around him a bunch of young, dedicated and talented performers willing to work for almost nothing. His first presentation was his own new play, *The Girls Next Door*. It was not his regular light fare, but a more serious effort, which he termed a psychological mystery.

He had hired the theater at Brighton for the tourist season, done some advertising in London, and now it looked as though he might get a boost from the famous Simon Cranston, producer of the most-watched talk show on British TV.

"It could be the making of us," Gus ran on, his bleary eyes alight with joy. "I knew Simon way back in the old days. I dropped him a couple of tickets in the mail, but I never imagined he'd actually show. I haven't seen him in years. He didn't even phone, just popped in after tonight's performance."

"That's wonderful, Gus. What a terrific break," Tillie congratulated him. "Do you want me to come along and decorate the set for you? It's too bad Jessie isn't here. She's the star of the show."

"Her own fault. She didn't want to pass up a date with her new friend. It's not every day the likes of Jessica Miter gets a date with a member of parliament, who is kin to lords and ladies," he finished on a sarcastic note.

"Where is Cranston? When does he want to do the interview?"

"He's out front with a film crew now. It's only a ten-minute spot for his nightly show. He usually does a culture bit at the end. Hard news, politics, whoever is in the headlines at the moment, comes first. Powder your nose, Tillie, and come out front. We're using the stage set as our backdrop. Five minutes—can you make yourself gorgeous in that time?"

"I can try," she answered. On a burst of excitement, she ran to Gus and hugged him. He was fiftyish and balding, and the younger actresses regarded him as a second father.

"It's just like the old days," he said, shaking his head and hurrying to the door. "I'll pour him a drink. Scotch . . . that's what he takes. Scotch on the rocks. He won't get the rocks tonight, but he'll like the Scotch, all right. My best."

Tillie closed the door, then turned to face the light-rimmed mirror. She was not accustomed to the luxury of actually sitting down at the dressing table. She shared the room with Jessie, who reserved the chair to herself. Jessie was a good actress, the most experienced of the troupe, and by far the most beautiful of the women there.

Gus called her "next year's blonde," a movie term referring to the annual appearance on movie and TV screens of a gorgeous blond sex symbol—not necessarily talented. These women would become big stars for a year or two, then people would get tired of looking at them, or the styles would change, or the blondes would marry millionaires and retire.

Jessie filled the bill perfectly. She had about two feet of hair bleached practically white, which waved in undulating profusion. She also had big blue eyes with long lashes, a cute nose, good teeth and the kind of figure that never went out of style with the men, whatever was happening with women's fashion magazines. She made no secret of the fact that she wanted a fast rise to fame, a fast marriage to money and a life of jetting to and fro with the beautiful people. Work was for slaves; she planned to do the minimum of it.

Tonight, Tillie had the mirror to herself. She looked at the face that looked back at her. She looked

frightened, pale and frightened. Her eyes were too
big; her face too white, too narrow; her mouth too
wide. Simon Cranston would think her ugly.

And what did it matter what Simon Cranston
thought of her? Just because she and every other
female in the country ogled him shamelessly for thirty
minutes a night, five nights a week, was no reason to
think he would think her anything special. He was
going to interview Gus about the play. It was a terrific
break for Gus; she'd sit and look as pretty as she could
for the ten minutes of the interview, speaking only if
spoken to.

She paused to consider things. She could at least
look like an actress—wear something outlandish. She
whipped off her cotton blouse and skirt, borrowed a
wildly flowered long gown of Jessie's and put it on. It
was loose and floating, so the size didn't matter. She
took her straight black hair, which was just hanging
down her back like a child's, and twisted it into a
chignon. Using the stage makeup before her on the
table, she drew black lines around her eyes, tilted the
lines up at the ends, smeared on some purple eye
shadow, rooted in the mess of the jewelry box for
dangling earrings and clipped them on. This done, she
stood back a few feet from the mirror to view the
result.

"Not too bad, if I do say so myself," she said to the
mirror. She looked like an actress, at least—which
was something she did not usually accomplish, even
on the stage. She played the plain one in the drama, a
foil for Jessica's blond magnificence. With her head
tilted to one side, she picked up Jessie's long cigarette
holder, couldn't find a cigarette for it, but took it
along with her anyway. She felt very glamorous and
very unlike herself as she set off for the stage.

Her heart beat rapidly as she passed along the corridor. There, two men were setting up lights, arranging mikes and talking to each other. She hardly glanced at them. Her eyes flew straight to Simon Cranston. He was every bit as handsome off the screen as on. He was tall and lithe, his face tanned from the sun—very probably not the English sun. Simon traveled all over the world to do his special documentaries, as well as his nightly show. Even during reruns, his ratings didn't suffer. A well-cut jacket, hanging open in the casual manner that was his trademark, covered his broad shoulders. He wore no tie, but a rather narrow gold chain with a lion suspended from it. All of his audience knew him for a Leo. His dark hair was worn a little long, with sideburns and a shock of straight black hair on top which tended to fall over his forehead. Tillie had a moment's privacy to admire his clean-cut profile: that familiar, classic nose that belonged on a Roman coin; that strong chin and firm jawline. Then he turned toward her, and she gave up thinking.

Television didn't do his eyes justice. It didn't show the mischievous sparkle, the light of interest when an attractive woman came on the scene. It didn't show how dangerously dark they were, nearly black.

"This must be your leading lady," Simon said, turning to Gus for an introduction.

"One of them. This is Tillie Brennan. She plays the bad girl in the play."

"She doesn't look bad to me," was Simon's appreciative reply. The words were nothing, commonplace. The expression was all. There was admiration in it, interest; there was even a hint of seduction. "Not bad at all," he added as he paced quickly toward her to take her hands in his. He held them as he smiled down at her.

"I imagine you recognize Simon Cranston, Tillie," Gus said.

"I've watched your show on TV for years, Mr. Cranston," she said, swallowing a gulp.

"Two insults in one sentence! Don't you teach your girls any manners, Gus? The name is *Simon,* as in 'Simple Simon,' not Mr. Cranston, and if you have been watching my show for more than three or four years, I would prefer not to hear about it. Have I really reached that time of gray eminence when beautiful young women tell me they have watched me for *years?*"

The stagehands made some laughing comments. "Seven years this autumn, Simon," one reminded him.

"Everybody's a mathematician. You're fired!" Simon said, also laughing. "Giving my secrets away. I broke into the business when I was nine or ten, Tillie," he joked. "May I call you Tillie?"

"Certainly," she answered, flustered.

They were directed to their seats—behind a coffee table that was part of the set. Mikes were attached and light meters brought out, giving Tillie time to assess Simon's likely age. Thirty, she decided. There were little wrinkles around the eyes; some fine lines in the forehead; even the beginning of a softness around the lips, which enhanced their sensual quality.

"We're in a hurry. Let's try to get it in one take," Simon said. "It doesn't matter if it's off the wall. I want an impromptu feel to it. I'll give you a puffing up, Gus, ask a few questions, then give you a chance to expound on your play. Okay?"

"Fine, Simon."

Lights blazed on, nearly blinding Tillie. Then, what a strange beginning! Simon reached across the table and offered her a cigarette. That was the beginning of the filmed interview. She didn't even smoke, but since she held Jessie's holder, she accepted the offer, inserted the cigarette and tried to light it while Simon's brown hand held the light steady.

Next, Simon turned to face the camera and began his prologue to the interview.

"This ravishing woman who smokes when she shouldn't is Miss Tillie Brennan, the star of *The Girls Next Door,* he said, in a playful vein. "Don't we wish *our* neighbors looked like this, gentlemen? Her play is on now at the Brighton Theater, and if you hustle, you can still get a ticket." He went on to give the location, time, and even the price—all of which he read from the theater card.

"You will, of course, remember Gus Brooks, on my left, the director of the play," he continued. "Gus is well remembered in London for his delightful, debonair drawing-room comedies, and I couldn't be happier he has done another. You authored this play yourself, Gus?"

"Yes . . . yes, I did," Gus answered, looking dazed. "But really—"

The reason for his bewilderment was that his new play was *not* at all one of the debonair Noel Cowardish things for which he used to be known. This work was much more serious. Jessie played the beautiful daughter; Tillie, the plain one. The audience's sympathy was for Tillie during most of the action, then, as the third act began, things shifted, revealing the plain daughter as a complete monster who is maneuvering to kill off her sister and steal her fiancé. Tillie's lines were fewer, her role purposely understated, so that her unscrupulousness would come as a shock. It was a challenging part, requiring subtle acting.

"We're really ready for one of those sophisticated comedies you do so well, Gus," Simon ran on. "I, for one, am filled to the teeth with heavy, turgid *drahma*," he said, pronouncing the last word with mock elegance. "And the summer-tourist set at Brighton will find it a welcome relief, too. Now, why don't we find out something about your star, Miss Tillie Brenner?"

"I—I'm not . . . it's not— Really, Mr. Cranston, you have got it all wrong," Tillie said, horrified at the incoherent sounds issuing from her mouth. He hadn't even got her name right!

"Don't tell me Gus has taken leave of his senses," Simon said, smiling fondly. "He wouldn't have found the most beautiful brunette since Liz Taylor and not made her his star. *I* certainly think you steal the show."

"I'm not the star," she said as the smoke curled from her cigarette and wafted into her eyes. She put it out and batted the smoke away.

"I warned you it was a bad habit," Simon said, with a laugh at her performance. "If you don't consider yourself the star, Miss Brenner, then how would *you* describe your role?"

"I play a devious woman, trying to steal my sister's fiancé. I don't think I should tell any more, or it will spoil it for the audiences still to come."

"The audience will be totally mystified that you have to *try* to steal a fiancé. It strikes me you wouldn't have to lift a finger to steal any man in the country. Why don't you steal me instead? I won't give you a bit of argument," he said, his eyes lingering fondly on her face.

Flirting with his female guests was not a new thing for Simon. It was a trick he often employed with great success. Perhaps it was some part of his charm, his appeal for women, these frequent displays of gallantry. Women like a man who likes women. Tillie had watched him play this role many times, but still she felt a flush of pleasure at being on the receiving end for once. It was almost like a daydream coming true.

"In . . . in the play, I am the plain one, you see," she explained, conscious again of her stuttering. "You must have mistaken me for Jessica, though I don't see how you could. She is the blonde."

"I never make that kind of mistake about ladies," he assured her easily. "What I said was that *I* think you steal the show. Every man is entitled to his opinion. My opinion is that we will see Tillie Brenner's name in lights before long."

"I hope they spell it right," Gus interposed. "The name is Brennan, not Brenner, Simon."

"I *do* beg your pardon. I just lose my head in the face of so much pulchritude, but a Tillie by any name is just as sweet. Now we must all make an effort to forget Miss Brennan and ask Gus Brooks about his play *The Girls Next Door*. This is its first presentation, is it, Gus?"

"Yes, I wrote it last year. It's a mystery, an old-fashioned mystery, but of course I can't give away any plot secrets."

"That's an unusual twist for you, adding mystery to your plays, isn't it? It sounds very clever. I expect the tone of it will be similar to Noel Coward's *Blithe Spirit*. Lots of witty repartee—"

"It's a new direction for me, a departure from the old style," Gus explained.

Simon listened carefully, to avoid making any further blunders. To review a play you hadn't seen was tricky, but to pretend you *had* seen it was downright foolhardy. Thank God it's only on tape he thought. Having pretended he had seen it, he now had to quickly revise the bent of his questions. "I realize that, and I'm sure it will be a great success. The comments overheard in the lobby were certainly favorable." This, at least, was true. He *had* arrived before the audience came out.

"They say the man who builds a better mousetrap will have the world beating a path to his door, and the man who writes a better *Mousetrap* will have audiences doing likewise. *The Mousetrap,* for those in our audience under five—or living locked in an ivory tower—is the longest-running play in England: a mystery, like Gus Brooks's new play. Why don't you give us some background on the people playing in it, Gus?"

For five minutes Gus expanded on his venture, answering careful, discreet questions from Simon. Tillie sat silent, decorating the set, very much aware of the host's eyes sliding often in her direction. As the ten-minute tape neared its end, the talk turned once more to the play, Simon again urging the audiences to hurry to Brighton to see a delightful new mystery-comedy starring Tillie Brennan as a vamp who specializes in stealing boyfriends from less attractive ladies. "Ladies: first and last," he said, winding up. "Let's give Tillie the last word."

Tillie looked at a confused, offended Gus. The great Simon Cranston had not understood the play. He was a fool, an incompetent fool; he was misleading people. They would come seeking comedy and be disappointed. Some might even think Gus *thought* he had written a comedy and think he had lost his touch completely. The great break was turning into a fiasco, and she had about fifty seconds in which to correct it.

She cast a dark scowl on Simon, took a deep breath and plunged in. Lights were flashing, giving some incomprehensible signal.

"I don't know what play Simon Cranston is recommending you see, but *I* highly recommend you come to see ours. It isn't a slick, sophisticated comedy. It isn't Shakespeare, either, or Agatha Christie, but we think it's good. The stars are Jessica Miter and Ron Beccles."

She spoke quickly, with worried looks at the man making motions with his hands to "wind it up."

Simon stared at her, unbelieving. Suddenly he jumped to his feet. "Cut! That's it! All over. Thank you for spoiling the interview, Miss Tillie Whoever-You-Are. Are you trying to make me look like a damned fool?" His eyes were blazing with anger, his whole body taut.

"No, Mr. Simon Whoever-You-Are, you don't need any help from *me!*"

"We can't use it. She spoiled the interview. Sorry, Gus. It would have been a good boost for your play, but . . . Next time, we'll try to get the star of the show to sit in, and hope she has a little more professionalism than this young lady."

Tillie looked at Gus, whose disappointment was easy to see, but as she turned back to Simon, his arrogant look brought her anger to the boil again. "Professionalism?" she asked, with a startled laugh. "An odd requirement on your part, surely? You're not much concerned with 'professionalism,' coming here with no advance notice to interview a play that was obviously over your head, giving people wrong ideas of what to expect."

"We're giving them the time and place and name. It's worth money in the bank, lady."

"Pity it couldn't have been the *right* name, in my case at least," she shot back angrily.

"I have a piece of advice for you, young lady. If you hope to make a name for yourself in this business, you don't start off by insulting people who can help you. I *could* have made you a household name, but that tape won't be shown, thanks to your childish outburst."

"Thanks to *your* incompetence, you mean. You wouldn't want your slavering audience to know how misinformed you are. The great Simon Cranston can't understand a straightforward play when he sees it. Too bad your research staff hadn't been along to explain it to you."

"See it? I didn't bother to see it. I have better things to do with my time. I happened to be in town and wanted to give an old friend's work a boost."

On this haughty speech, he turned his back on her and spoke to his crew. Then he expressed his regret to Gus, and left.

Tillie followed Gus to his office. "I'm sorry. I blew it pretty good, didn't I? I should have kept quiet, but to hear him misrepresenting your play . . . That review would have done more harm than good."

"It's all right, Tillie. Simon has long pride and a short fuse, but he settles down soon after he explodes. He might reconsider later on and come back."

"I hope so."

The bottle of Scotch sat on Gus's desk, unopened. Either Simon had declined, or there hadn't been time to offer him a drink. Gus looked at it with decided interest. He was no longer an alcoholic, but unlike some of them, he trusted himself for a little drinking. He rationed himself to one or two drinks a day, and only after working hours.

"I was surprised to see him here at all," Tillie

mentioned. "He usually does bigger stories. A new play at the National Theatre, for instance. Actors like Olivier or Gielgud or Richardson. Was he a good friend of yours before, Gus?"

"Not really. I met him a few times around the theater, or at parties. I'm surprised he knew I was opening this week. I put a small ad in the *Times*, but it was easy to overlook. It took me five minutes to find it. We didn't get any reviews in London. This could have been the break—a chance to play the West End. Oh well, time for my medicine," he said, reaching for the bottle.

"You won't forget the dosage?" she asked, worried.

"I can't. If I have more than two, I don't let myself touch a drop for a month. It keeps me in line. Want a shot?"

"No, thanks."

He poured one into the glass and sipped it neat. "I hardly recognized you when you came out front," he said, looking at Tillie's outfit. "You give next year's blonde a run for her money in that getup. Whose is it?"

"Next year's blonde's. She'll sue me if she finds out I borrowed it. At least she won't see me in it on TV. Too bad she wasn't here. Who is this new fellow she's seeing? He's the member of parliament, I take it?"

"That's right. Charles Greville. She hired a rowboat this week for the purpose of capsizing at the end of his dock. He took her home to his ancestral heap to dry her out. She barely arrived in time for the curtain. He was in the audience tonight. On a free ticket, unfortunately," Gus added unhappily.

"What's he like?"

"Very upper-class, old boy sort of thing, don'tcha know," Gus replied, lifting his thumb and index finger to his eye like a monocle and looking down his nose through the circle formed. "Sister married to a lesser lord; decaying mansion two or three hundred years old; family the same age and state of decrepitude. He lives in London. He's rusticating at his place on the west side of Brighton. In a spot of trouble, if rumor serves."

"What kind of trouble?" she asked, her interest quickening.

"Money trouble, political trouble. His career will be scuppered if he really had his fingers in the cookie jar. Only a few rumors have leaked out, but I believe his own party, the Tories, are looking into his affairs. They've sent him down here to get him out of the public eye for a spell, then he'll quietly retire and save them a great thundering scandal."

"Was he on the take—involved in some sort of bribery?"

"It is whispered he gave some road-paving contract to friends of his, *not* the lowest bidders, but of course that doesn't prove anything. It's not necessarily the lowest bid that should get the contract, if their work is of poor quality. We seem to have got the worst of both worlds with the Honorable Charles Greville: a good stiff price, and pavement that is already crumbling after two years. So far it's all innuendo. I know no harm of the man, except that he has a face like an ostrich."

"He hardly sounds the sort Jessica would be bothered with."

"He wears the right tie—old school. Belongs to the proper clubs, goes to the right parties. A bit of a swinger, Charles. He could get her name and face in the papers. I'm sure she doesn't consider him anything other than a lower rung of the ladder she's climbing."

"She could have taken a longer stride upward

tonight if she had been here to meet Simon Cranston."

"Very true. Simon is not averse to a pretty face, providing it is perched atop an equally pretty body. He's a leg man, however, and Jess has fat ankles. I wouldn't be surprised if she rings him up and tells him how sorry she is she missed his visit. She could persuade him to return. She talked *me* into adding several pages of scintillating dialogue for her, at the risk of upsetting the harmony of the play—to say nothing of the other actors who wanted the lines for themselves."

Tillie felt a stab of annoyance at the hint that Jessie could conciliate Cranston after she had had the stupidity to anger him. However, there was no denying Jessica had a way with men, and the play's success was so important to the whole troupe that Tillie didn't express displeasure with the notion.

She left Gus's office to return to her dressing room and remove her makeup, slip out of Jessica's robe and get back into her own cotton skirt and blouse. She left her hair up, shrugged into her denim jacket that matched her skirt, and went out by the stage door. There were no stage-door Johnnys standing around. Why had she thought Simon Cranston might be there waiting for her, waiting to apologize? He had even said he was in a hurry. He would be dashing off to meet some beautiful girl, someone like Jessica Miter. Probably went right back to London, in fact, where he belonged.

She managed to put him out of her thoughts as she showered, put on a pot of water to boil for tea, then tidied her little cubbyhole that was jokingly described as a "kitchen" by the landlady. The members of the troupe did not live at Gus's tumbledown house. There might have been room, but women liked the convenience of more than one bath for twenty people. They also preferred the small city of Brighton, lively in summer with tourists, to the lonely countryside. With a summer season's work guaranteed, Tillie had settled into a small apartment, preferring to live alone rather than share with others.

She eagerly looked forward to this summer. The current play was to run for three weeks, followed by one of Gus's older West End comedies for the next two. During August, they were to present a Feydeau farce, finishing the last half of the month with *The Rivals*, an eighteenth-century comedy by Richard Brinsley Sheridan, a tried and true classic.

It was good experience. Positions in London were hard to come by, and for anyone who could not *live* without being in the theater, this was just fine. For Tillie, the acting was not of prime importance. Like Gus, she was interested in the whole craft of the theater. She wanted to write and direct, and a little acting experience was a help, too. It showed you more clearly than just reading or seeing a play what pacing was all about. She was coming to recognize what speeches read well but spoke poorly. The sound of the words was important—The soft and harsh syllables must be used in the right places, or a mood could be destroyed. Some sounds were inherently silly, others important-sounding. The kind of dialogue also affected the mood—A long speech by one person was an entirely different matter from several short speeches by two or more characters. The way the words were said could also change the whole mood and meaning.

At times, she wished she could be on the stage performing and still out front with the director, absorbing it all at one time. She was acting in only two of the four productions. On the last, she was being allowed to direct, with of course, generous help from Gus. She devoted most of her time and attention to this challenge. When she curled up in bed half an hour later, she had her copy of *The Rivals* with her, pen in hand, to make notes, underline a bit here or there, jot down a question to ask Gus. Jessie was to play the ingenue in the play—Lydia Languish. It seemed to her poor casting, but Gus didn't have a lot of choices. And if she told him she disapproved, she feared he would make her play the role herself. Jessie was prone to overacting. The broad stroke was her style; she had very little subtlety.

It wasn't till she put the book aside and turned out her light that she thought again of Simon Cranston. It was too bad she had burst out and spoiled the interview, but really he was impossible. She simply couldn't keep her temper while he strutted about, blaming *her* for the terrible botch *he* had made of it. She had never thought from watching him on TV that he would be so self-important. He seemed to be lively and witty, almost self-deprecating at times, swift to admit a mistake. Now she knew why. He just didn't air his real mistakes. What a comfortable way to live—to erase your errors. That wasn't possible on the stage. If you goofed, everyone knew it at once. She mustn't goof on *The Rivals,* which meant she must curb Jessica's style. It seemed hopeless, so she thought of other things.

Simon Cranston again popped into her head. Her first thought of phoning him and apologizing was soon gone. She wouldn't bow and scrape to him, or to anyone. She had more pride than that. If Jessie wanted to do it, let her go ahead. She and Simon would get along just fine.

But then again, Simon had seemed very much taken with *her*. She didn't look like Liz Taylor, did she? No, not at all. And she didn't usually wear exaggerated clothes and makeup, either. That's what he had liked: Jessie's gown and stage makeup. He liked fast, painted women, ones who kept their mouths shut.

Chapter Two

When Jessie Miter came into the dressing room actually smiling and humming next day, Tillie wondered why. She couldn't have heard that she had missed out on meeting Simon Cranston the night before; that much at least was certain. Gus, the chicken, had been afraid to tell her, or perhaps he had told her, and she had phoned Simon and . . . In the batting of an eye, Tillie imagined a whole scenario in which Jessie and Simon were going out together.

"Guess what," Jessie said, smiling in a way that produced two large dimples, one smack in the middle of either cheek.

"You won the Irish sweepstakes," Tillie answered.

"Better. Charles Greville's sister has invited me to Lonsmere for the weekend. They were visiting Charles today at his place. I was there for tea. Lonsmere is her estate in Kent, my deah, in case you are unaware of the stately homes of England. She's a

28

baroness—Lady Travers. Isn't it lovely? I wonder who all will be there. Besides me and Charles, I mean."

"I hope you aren't planning to go before Saturday's evening performance, Jessie."

"Of course not. Charles is picking me up tomorrow night after it, in his Mercedes. We are motoring straight through to Lonsmere, and will be in time for the tail end of a super party she's tossing that night."

While Jessica was in this state of euphoria, it seemed a good time to tell her about Simon's visit the night before. Tillie did so, with all proper emphasis on her own unfortunate outbreak.

"Damn! I wish I'd been here," Jessie exclaimed, her pretty face coloring in vexation. "Simon Cranston, imagine! He could make a girl rich and famous. He has terrific prestige. His show is so popular. Was he really angry about the interview?"

"Angry with me for spoiling it," Tillie confessed. "I don't mind losing the air time myself, but I *do* feel bad for Gus's sake. Gus thinks Simon might simmer down and come back another night. So be sure you don't change your mind and skip off to Lonsmere before the play."

"I'm a professional, dear. You don't have to coach *me*."

Just how "professional" three minor parts in relatively minor plays made her was a moot point, and one not discussed in front of her face. It was professional enough to give her first turn at the mirror, in any case. Tillie edged her way to its outer corner to finish her own makeup while Jessie adroitly ran lipstick over her full lips, drawing the line just a hair's breadth beyond their natural edge, to enhance their size and fullness.

"Do you really think he'll come back?" Jessie asked when she had finished this important operation.

"I don't know. Gus thinks he might."

"I wish he'd come tonight. I don't have a date tonight. Charles has some business meeting. I'm going to ask Bennie to keep an eye out for Simon and let me know if he comes."

She darted out the door to call Bennie, the curly-headed adolescent who had been struck down with stage fever, and spent all his time hanging around the Brighton Theater—doing odd jobs and running for coffee, papers or food.

"He's not here, but it's a full house, at least," she said when she returned. It was two minutes to curtain, that tingling time when frayed nerves stretched taut; when conversation was reduced to monosyllables; when Tillie sat with her fingers crossed, rehearsing her first speech, and Jessie went to the wings, taking deep breaths to calm herself, or possibly to excite the stagehands.

The next hour and a half passed in a kind of dream state, the only link with reality that sea of indistinguishable, white, floating faces in the hall. The performance went well. It was sparked by Jessica's high spirits. She was the star, her role the most important and the most difficult—at least in terms of length of lines. When she was in good form, everyone responded. On such nights, Tillie understood the lure of the stage. Performing would never be her own career— She hadn't the iron nerves for it—but she could understand the thrill it gave the others. It was exhilarating, but it was also exhausting. As soon as it was over, the curtain calls taken, Tillie usually went straight home.

Some of the others were going to a nearby tavern to have a few beers and rehash the night's show, but Tillie said that she felt too tired. The others wouldn't have to be back till next afternoon to rehearse another play. Tillie would need to be there in the morning as well, to discuss with Gus the direction of *The Rivals,* to badger and pester the wardrobe mistress and generally learn all she could about all aspects of her craft. She would even learn how to work the lights. She stayed behind when the others left in a group, in order to talk to Gus about her ideas for the appearance of Mrs. Malaprop in what they called "her" play.

But Gus was busy with the perpetual balance sheet, and hadn't time for her. With a yawn, she went along the darkened corridor, out the stage door to take the brisk walk to her flat, which was only three blocks away.

She noticed the dark gleam of a car parked to the left. Charles must have come for Jessica after all, she thought, noticing that it was expensive, but not able to discern its make. She took a step toward it, to tell him that Jessie had already left. As she approached, a tall, lithe form emerged from the car. Charles had a better outline than she had expected—taller, wider shoulders. Then, as the man strode into the light from the overhead streetlamp, she realized her error. It wasn't Charles. It was Simon Cranston, and he was waiting for *her.* Her heart beat faster, causing a sensation not unlike first-night jitters. Funny, she hadn't been that breathless when she went before the TV camera for the interview. But then, she hadn't met him before that time, didn't know how he used his eyes. He hadn't called her beautiful and said all sorts of complimentary things to her. And she hadn't lashed out at him, either.

He pulled a white handkerchief from his breast pocket and waved it. "White flag of truce," he said, cocking his head to one side and smiling. "It's not the thing to shoot the enemy when he's carrying one," he pointed out. "It's against the Geneva Convention, or something."

"As luck would have it, I forgot to bring my gun tonight," she answered lightly.

"Isn't that *always* true when you meet the folks you'd like to shoot?" he asked.

"It never fails," she agreed, relieved to see he was in a friendly mood.

"I guess you know why I'm here," he said, stuffing the handkerchief back into his pocket.

"To see Gus? He'll be—"

"No, to see *you,* Miss Tillie Brennan. It *is* 'Miss,' I hope? I've had a long drive for nothing if it isn't."

"I prefer Ms.," she said, "but I'm not married, if that's what you meant. Funny, a few years ago it was the women who used to ask that question."

"Some of them still do—the ones who call themselves Miss. I am always at pains to let them know I'm available. But whether it is Ms., Miss or Mrs., I came to apologize for last night's inexcusable behavior. I have decided to blame it on the moon. There was a full moon. It always turns me into a jackass."

"Hmm, it's still full enough to be having some little effect," she said, looking up at the white circle that rode high overhead.

"So it is. By the last quarter, you will find me a much better behaved fellow," he promised. "Can I take you home, or better, take you to some quiet bar and ply you with alcohol and compliments?"

Her fatigue was gone, dissipated by his exciting presence. She would have said Yes even if she hadn't wanted to hint him into giving Gus that boost on his TV show.

"You can omit the compliments, but a gin and tonic would be appreciated," she answered, letting him take her elbow to lead her toward his car. "Nice," she said, staring in the darkness to discover the make. "Is it . . . is it *really* a Rolls-Royce, Mr. Cranston?" she asked, her voice rising.

"I wouldn't be caught dead in such a *nouveau riche* buggy, Ms. Brennan. It's a Bentley."

"Oh," she said, sliding onto the leather seat as he held the door for her.

"Where would you like to go, Ms. Brennan?" he asked, lifting a brow to let her know he was going to go on calling her Ms. Brennan till she called him Simon.

"The kids all go to Nick's Tavern," she said. "It's just down—"

"Thank you for the warning. We'll go to The George, shall we?"

"It's all right with me," she agreed, impressed in spite of herself. The George was an elite hotel that Tillie had thus far seen only from the outside.

He slid the car into reverse, backed out quickly, turned around and nosed onto the street, taking the correct turn at the corner. He was obviously no stranger to the seaside city.

"I'm not really dressed for The George," she mentioned, glancing down at her denim skirt and regretting she was not in a higher style for this momentous occasion.

"You shouldn't be. You should be dressed for Simon. Ladies should dress to please their escorts, don't you think? Or have the Ms. set cast that custom by the boards too, Ms. Brennan?"

"All right, Simon. I get the hint. You can stop calling me Ms. And we still dress to please men we're trying to impress, even the Ms.'s among us."

"Good girl," he said, reaching in the darkness to pat her fingers. His hand was warm. "You look fine, by the way. The crowd I saw before the show were all tourists, dressed in whatever wrinkled rags they found at the bottoms of their suitcases."

"Did you see the show?" she asked, startled.

"Why, yes. A certain young lady hinted the other night it might be a good idea for me to do so, before reviewing it. Brenner, I think her name was. You wouldn't know her. A bad-natured little wench, but uncommonly pretty."

He pulled up to the front of the hotel. The parking attendant came toward him. "Don't put it too far away. I'll be taking my friend home later," Simon told him.

"You're staying here overnight, are you?" she asked.

"Yes, I'm hoping for a late night. I'm an optimist," he answered with a devastating smile. It started at the eyes and traveled slowly down to his lips. He took her hand in his, and together they walked into the lobby.

Heads turned as customers recognized him. There were whispers, one pointing out this illustrious personage among them to another, as Simon walked Tillie quickly toward the bar.

"Is it always this bad?" she asked.

"No, sometimes it's worse. People push pieces of paper under your nose, demanding signatures. I'm always afraid it might be a check, or a confession of murder."

The waiter came toward them, bowing. "Good evening, Mr. Cranston. I enjoyed your show this evening. Can I help you?"

"Thanks, Jacob. Have you got a nice dark table for two?"

They were led to the back, hidden in a corner. A candle in an old miner's lamp twinkled through a brass jacket, but as Tillie's eyes became accustomed to the darkness, she could make out her partner's features.

"That looks like a genuine antique—one of Davy's safety lamps," he said, picking the object up. "A fairly simple contraption to have saved numerous lives," he commented, replacing it. "A gin and tonic, I think you said? We'll make it two, please."

The waiter bowed and left. Simon leaned comfortably against the leather-padded seat, joined his hands together to form a cathedral and stared at her till she began to wonder if there was something the matter with her face.

"Shall I go and powder my nose?" she asked.

"By all means, if you think it necessary. We wouldn't want any embarrassing accidents. I believe you'll find the ladies' room just—"

"You idiot! I didn't mean *that!* You were staring at me so hard I thought I must look horrible or something."

"That's not what I was staring at. I was just wondering where Miss Brenner went. What happened to her elegant coiffure, her flowing gown, her make-up? I don't even see her cigarette holder this evening. That getup cannot have been your stage makeup. I have seen the play now, and you were *you,* so who the devil was Miss Brenner?"

"Oh, is that what you were looking for? Well, if you really must know—"

"Yes, I want to know everything about you," he said simply, as though he meant it. It did peculiar things to her feelings.

"This is me. The glamorous actress you found so uncommonly pretty was an actress Gus invited to sit in for the interview, to lend it a touch of show-biz glitter.

Glamour, you know. 'Set decoration,' he called it. I don't believe the decoration was supposed to have a speaking part. I'm sorry about last night."

"What's that awfully corny line from the movie? 'Love is never having to say,' et cetera. But then we're not in love yet, are we?"

She had the queasy sensation of being at the brink of it. In approximately fifteen minutes, he had taken her opinion of him and turned it completely upside down. He was not arrogant at all. He was charming, dangerously charming. He was lively, fun, and had cared enough to come down from London just to apologize. "Not yet. I never fall in love on the first date."

"I never did before, either."

The drink came to her rescue, saving Tillie from having to speak when her heart was hammering in her throat. She gulped it quickly, and fell into a fit of coughing.

"I see you drink the same way you smoke," he commented. "How refreshing. Am I a cockeyed optimist to hope you are what my mother calls a 'nice, old-fashioned girl'?"

"I'd have to know your mother before I answered that, Simon."

"That could be arranged. But let's not rush things. We hardly know each other yet."

"I didn't mean . . . that . . . anything."

"A novel admission. You women usually let on you *do* mean something, no matter what babble is coming out of your mouths. I realize it was not a hint for me to call up the preacher, dart out and buy a diamond. I also realize you haven't answered my question."

"I don't smoke. I do take a social drink. I am not a dope addict, nor do I have a slew of lovers. I don't know whether that makes me a 'nice, old-fashioned girl.'"

"I can't imagine why the admission should make you an angry one. You are being subjected to my highest caliber of charm, Tillie. You should be smiling by now, telling me you have seen and admired me on TV for three or four years, but not a *second* longer. That you have profited from the wit and wisdom of my column might be mentioned; that would give me the opportunity to tell you my career plans. We men all like to talk about ourselves, you know."

"I suppose I already know quite a bit about your career, and it's more than plans. You already have a TV show and a daily newspaper column. What more plans can you possibly have?"

He hunched his shoulders. "Being a celebrity is fun, but the glamour wears off after a while. A man wants to be remembered for something more than doing a talk show and a high-class gossip column."

"Your column is more than that," she objected quickly. "You do those political pieces, news background. I always read your 'Simon Says.' Everybody does."

"Thank you, but I'd like to do more. I'm working on a book, a serious book. Not a novel, but a sort of social history, with background on how we as a country got into the mess we're in. I have all the ideas, and I *think* I have the talent and determination to see it through. What I lack is time."

"There never seems to be enough time for anything," she agreed.

"I should think an actress would have plenty of time to herself, once the play was actually running. Your rehearsals must be over; you have your days to yourself, at least."

"Oh no! We have the other three plays to prepare. I'm directing the last one," she added proudly.

"I didn't realize Gus had organized a whole repertory company," he said with interest. "We must be sure to work that into the next interview."

"Oh, you're going to do another!" she exclaimed. "I'm so glad, for Gus's sake. He's worked like a dog on this project, and sunk every penny he owns into it, too."

They talked easily, he expanding on his intended book, she telling him her plans. They had another gin and tonic, and still had so much to say to each other that neither of them mentioned how late it was getting.

It was one o'clock, the bar thinning of customers, and still they talked on. She had long since forgotten that he was famous. Once in a rare while, you meet a person, of the same sex or the opposite, who seems a kind of soul mate. Your most confused utterances are understood without long explanation. You like the same books and plays and jokes. The talk ranges easily from politics to religion to a silly sitcom that you both admit, with some embarrassment, to liking. You feel, in an evening, as if you had known the person all your life. That was how Tillie felt with Simon. It was also impossible to overlook the very striking fact that he was of the opposite sex and extremely attractive.

"There should be some good seafood in Brighton," he said suddenly. "I'm famished. How about you?"

"I could eat a small horse. But it's getting late. Everything will be closed."

"If we put the pedal to the floor, we can get out to the Nelson Inn before they lower the mainsail. They have marvelous shrimp, and a lobster that should be in the *Guinness Book of Records*. Shall we go?"

He finished off his drink, signed the bill, and they

hurried out. He did not quite keep the pedal to the floor, but did exceed the legal limit by more miles an hour than was quite comfortable. But he was a good driver, even with one hand holding hers. The car radio played a gooey, sentimental tune that suited her mood. She knew it would always remind her of this magical night.

"Henceforth, that will be *our* song," he told her, squeezing her fingers. "We can allow ourselves that one lapse into bad taste."

It was almost as if he had read her mind. "We have nothing to say about it. Some disc jockey must take the blame. How could he know we would have preferred Beethoven's Fifth?"

The lobster was as good as promised: fat, juicy, chewy morsels reluctant to leave the shell. The clarified butter melted into its crevices, tasting as one imagined nectar must taste. As they wrestled with shell crackers and long-tined forks, Simon said, "This fellow deserves champagne," and ordered it.

"You're extravagant," she scolded familiarly.

"Some evenings merit champagne. This is definitely a champagne evening."

"I wish I had been wearing a beautiful gown tonight," she said, yawning and feeling completely happy. Her head spun ever so slightly. She was sated with food and drink, and she was falling in love.

"I enjoy my happiest hours when I'm not dressed up. You wore a beautiful gown last night. Did you have a better time?"

"No. A beastly time."

"There you are, then. Shall we tackle the dance floor?"

At such an hour, the musicians were too tired to play raucous music, and the patrons too sleepy to dance to it so they played soft, sentimental ballads.

Simon took her in his arms. She placed her spinning head on his shoulder and sighed luxuriously. He held her close, moving rhythmically, slowly, talking little. His grip on her tightened as they moved, till, as they swayed to and fro, she could feel not only his hard chest against her but even his thighs.

His lips came down to her ear. "I can't wait much longer to kiss you, Tillie. Shall we go—or scandalize the patrons by doing it here?"

"You have a reputation to protect. We'd better go," she answered.

He kissed her as soon as they got into the car. He slid over to her side to escape the wheel, and pulled her into his arms for a deep, passionate embrace that sent her spinning head into orbit. It *was* magic. There was no other word for the luxurious, velvet feeling that had surrounded this whole evening, and most especially this kiss. Was it really possible she was in Simon Cranston's arms being told, though not verbally, that she was loved? Reluctantly, he moved over to his own side; but, with his arm around her waist, he pulled her with him. He asked directions to her apartment, and found it without difficulty.

"Would you like to come in for some coffee?" she asked, reluctant to see the evening end.

"I would, but I don't trust myself. You've already warned me you never fall in love on the first date. Unless you'd care to consider last night's fiasco a date?" he ventured with a smile.

"*Coffee* was what I offered, Simon."

"Oh, but I assumed you meant for breakfast. That's when I usually take my coffee."

"I serve decaffeinated after dark."

"What a ravishing, thoughtful, beautiful, desirable woman you are!" he exclaimed, encircling her tightly in his arms.

His lips were hot on hers. She was uneasy over his last few speeches, but as the pressure of his lips fired her, she forgot their innuendo. She felt only a rising tide of response to his embrace. When she felt his hands move in the close darkness of the car to caress her, she did not push him away, but enjoyed the softly sensual feel of his strong fingers gently stroking, exploring, arousing her to passion. His tongue eased her lips open to claim her mouth in a symbolic victory that he savored lengthily. The excitement of this intimacy warned her she should stop him soon, *at once*. But stopping this heady, luxurious adventure was the last thing she wanted to do. She wished it could continue till the sun rose. He lifted his head— only to lower his lips to her eyes, her ears, causing a tingling sensation deep within her.

"You adorable woman. Quite sure you never fall in love on the first date?" he asked, his voice husky, breathless, in her ear. "You wouldn't regret it."

"What does that mean?"

"I'm not a hit-and-run guy, here today and gone tomorrow. I think we could have something good together. We're both in the same kind of business. I could help your career—"

It was like a dash of cold water in her face. She jerked away, pushing him back from her violently. "You're offering to *buy* me. I may be in show biz, but I'm not in any other business. And even if I wanted to get ahead by *that* means, you're the last . . ." She came to an angry, confused stop, fighting back tears.

"Sorry!" he said, tossing up his hands like a criminal submitting to justice. "*You're* the one asked me in for coffee, remember? What's a guy to think?"

Her hands twitched with the desire to slap him. Here she thought he had been falling in love like her, when all he had in mind was some sleazy relationship.

She was a romantic fool. Jessica had told her so often enough. It was pointless to blame Simon for her naïveté—and foolish to voice all her outrage when he was still in a position to help Gus and the troupe.

"Sorry if I misled you," she said, trying not to sound too angry, though not pretending to be happy, either. "There are still a few corners of Merrie Olde England where a cup of coffee means a cup of coffee. I'm the old-fashioned kind, remember? Let's forget it."

"Oh, no. But we'll discuss it another time, when we're both sober. Completely sober, I mean. I don't know about you, but my head is behaving very poorly, and my heart isn't quite in sync, either. See you tomorrow. 'Luxurious lobster-nights farewell, For sober, studious days.' That's from an unfashionable poet named Pope, if you're interested in trivia. I'm a fiend for it, myself."

The world settled down with a dull thump. Simon was being himself again. She doted on trivia, too. Wasn't it too bad their similarities of taste had not extended to more important areas of life—such as sex and marriage?

"I have libraries on the subject," she answered, trying to sound natural.

"We'll subject each other to a quiz next time we meet."

He got out, opened her door, and walked with her to the outer door of her apartment building. There was a moment of awkwardness just as he was about to leave. He bent down, kissed the tip of her nose and said, "Keep my coffee warm. I shall return."

"General MacArthur, when he left the Philippines," she said, laughing in spite of her disappointment.

"Give the lady the prize," he said, bowing. "This is

the prize," he added, sweeping her into his arms for a last, quick, delicious kiss. He walked quickly to his car, turned on the motor and sped away with a hand in the air to wave farewell.

She emitted a sigh of regret and mounted the stairs to her third-story flat, suddenly aware of how very tired she was, and of how early eight o'clock would come. Only five hours of sleep!

It was closer to four by the time she rethought the evening, and decided she'd been a fool and Simon a charming scoundrel. Scoundrels shouldn't be allowed to be so charming. There should be a natural law that scoundrels be ugly, preferably deformed, and hideously unattractive—instead of like Simon.

Chapter Three

Eight o'clock came too early. Tillie shook herself from the pillow, punched down the alarm button and closed her eyes again. It was Saturday; she could go in an hour later. She was often there before Gus. She was her own hardest taskmaster. When next she opened her eyes, it was somehow ten o'clock. She felt first a sense of disappointment when she remembered the evening before, then as she thought of the good news she had for Gus, she felt better. At least she had controlled her temper this time. The interview was still on.

She made coffee—instant to save time—and was reminded again of Simon's remarks about when he took his coffee. She wondered how often, and with whom, he had taken it in the morning, after spending the night in some willing woman's bed. She thought, too, how interesting it would be to have him across the narrow table from her now, laughing, joking, talking, educating her in such a painless way. He had been so many places, done so many things, yet he would listen to her less-informed ideas with seeming pleasure. He hadn't made her feel stupid or ignorant.

How long a relationship had he had in mind? she wondered. A week, a month, a year? No, not a year. Simon changed women more often than that. He was society's darling playboy, having a fling with some of each year's debutantes, actresses, more prominent new writers, TV personalities, even the nobility. A month, she decided, would have been the duration. Long enough to have advanced her career in some fashion, introduced her to a few people who could help her. It was Jessica he should have taken out.

She brushed her long, black hair back, then remembering that it had looked good the night she pinned it up, she rolled it into a loose twist and pinned it to her head, where it felt uncomfortable but looked nice. She appeared more mature and sophisticated than when it hung loose. She slipped into a blue-and-white striped seersucker skirt, hastily buttoned a navy blouse and regarded herself in the mirror. Knowing that Simon might be there for the interview, she added a gold chain and earrings, and wore her high-heeled sandals to show off her trim ankles. She felt very chic. If she was to be a set decoration again, she might as well look her best.

She hoped Simon would do the interview in the morning, before Jessica arrived. The first person she met though, when she arrived, was Jessie Miter in a high state of glee.

"I *met* him!" she said, her eyes cast up to the heavens.

It wasn't necessary to ask whom, but Tillie humored her and asked anyway.

"Simon Cranston. Isn't he a doll? He's taking me out for lunch. He was asking for you, Tillie. He thought you might be here for the interview, but Gus and I did it. It went great. It won't be on till Monday. Be sure you watch for it."

"I wouldn't miss it. I'm glad it went so well," she said, swallowing her disappointment and anger. "Taking you out for lunch, did you say?"

"Yes. I've got to get out of that weekend with Charles if Simon asks me out tonight."

"Has he left the theater?" Tillie asked, her jaw tightening.

"No, he's having a chat with Gus. Gus is trying to twist his arm into doing a few more shows, sort of a running thing throughout the summer, you know. At least one segment on each of the new plays as it's presented. He was not at all averse to the idea. *I* suggested it," she added, looking into the mirror to stroke her hair.

"That would be wonderful," Tillie said, trying to feel some enthusiasm for this project. Simon did sometimes follow a project on his show and do three or four follow-up shows on it, so it was not entirely out of the question that he might do so here.

"I got to announce all the roles I play. He laughed out loud when he heard I am to do Lydia Languish in your play, Tillie. I told him—and the few million viewers—to come and see for themselves that I *am* an actress, as well as a sexpot."

"Did you actually say that on TV?"

"Tune in Monday and see for yourself. Where shall I have him take me for lunch? I want to be seen. I wish there were time to go to London."

"There's a nice seafood place about ten miles down

the coast. The Nelson Inn it's called, after the famous admiral. They have a good lobster," Tillie suggested masochistically.

"I like lobster, but it doesn't like me. I break out in welts, so it will have to be steak. It's not every day I date a guy who can afford it, though I must say Charles is liberal in his spending. He takes me to the Beefeater, a fabulous place."

She turned from the mirror to thumb through the outfits she kept in the dressing room for after-theater dates. She held various dresses up in front of her. She finally selected a floating peach-colored gown that hugged her body down past her hips and then swirled out into a full skirt. It was the bane of Jessie's life that she was required to wear a bra. "When you're built in the old-fashioned way like me, you need all the support you can get," she admitted, not too unhappily. She began brushing her hair, pulling it this way and that to decide what suited the mood she wished to create.

"I want to look like a star, not an ingenue," she explained to Tillie. "Simon's older. He won't be impressed by sweet innocence. How do you like this?" she asked, piling most of her hair on top of her head, with a few wanton curls falling about her ears in front.

"I imagine he'll like it," Tillie said, her accents clipped.

"Now, don't sulk, darling," Jessie said over her shoulder. "I might let you have Charles. You're refined enough to appeal to his snobbishness. Would you be interested in going out with him tonight, if Simon asks me out?"

"No, thanks. He's not my type."

"What *is* your type? I've never discovered the secret yet. Ron Beccles used to ask you out—He's cute. If you're really interested in your career, however, the type you should be concentrating on is the type that can do you some good. Really, Tillie, a girl has to do all she can to get ahead."

"We have different ideas about how a career should be advanced, I guess."

"We'll see who gets to the top first, you or me. What *I* have going for me is my looks, and an ounce of talent. And of course, a very *warm* personality."

"Don't forget to come back this afternoon, Jessie. We're going to run through the first act of my play."

"Oh, Tillie, couldn't you do the parts I'm not in today? Simon might— Well, there's no saying what might come up after a couple of drinks."

"Very true. If you're not here, I'll know what kept you, and we'll work on something else—something you're not in."

"Thanks a million. I've got to dash. I wouldn't want to keep the big man waiting."

She gave herself a quick spray from the perfume bottle that rested on her dressing table and darted out the door.

Tillie sat in front of the mirror, silently comparing the image to the one that had just left it. I guess I can say good-bye to Simon, she thought. He's not going to remember me when he has a beautiful, willing woman like Jessie to amuse him. It didn't take him long to ask her out. After a couple of drinks, it wouldn't take him long to go back with her to her apartment, either. She didn't expect to see Jessie at the afternoon rehearsal. She waited till she heard Jessie's voice, raised in excited chatter to Simon, pass the door and go down the hall to the exit before she went out front.

Gus was smiling, telling the troupe of their great luck. Simon had agreed to come back and do an interview for their next production.

"Leave it to Jessie," Ron Beccles, the leading man, said.

"You've lost her, Ron," another jeered.

"You mean Charles Greville has lost her. Jessie sheds guys like a snake sheds skins—no other comparison intended. I wonder why a snake cropped into my head?"

"I can't imagine," Gus answered. "A bird of paradise is more like it, in that golden-orange skin she had on when she went out."

There was some good-natured banter, then Gus sauntered over to Tillie. "Simon was asking for you, Tillie. I understand it's his fault you overslept today. He told me not to fire you, so I won't," he added, laughing.

"Kind of him," she answered, her tone snippy.

"I wouldn't worry too much about him and Jess, if that's what's troubling you."

"I'm not worried about *him*. It's Act Three of my play that's bugging me."

"Act Three will be flattered you got so dressed up to worry about it," he told her, undeceived. "It was just by chance that Jessie was here this morning for the interview. I didn't call her, you know. She dropped around to pick up her bikini, and saw his car in the car park. Whoever she had a date with has been left waiting. She didn't take time to phone and cancel her date. I wonder if it's Charles who is cooling his heels somewhere. She dropped his prestigious name into the conversation—quite accidentally, you understand—ten or twelve times, causing Simon to wink in amusement. She has all the subtlety of a carnival barker."

"About Act Three, Gus," she said determinedly, then went on to outline her problem.

The name Simon fell from their conversation, but

not from her mind. She kept a close watch on the door to see if Jessie returned for rehearsal. She didn't. She barely arrived in time to change for the evening performance.

"That was a long date," Tillie said, standing back from the mirror when she arrived. Tillie's makeup and costume were already in place. "I was afraid you weren't going to make it."

"I nearly didn't. We went to London, the *Savoy!* Oh Tillie, what bliss! He introduced me to a movie director and two actors. I nearly *died.*"

While Tillie rapidly calculated whether there had been time for a quick dash to a hotel in this busy day, Jessie spoke on. "I saw his apartment. Fabulous. All done in suede and chrome by an interior designer. Just like something out of a movie set."

"It sounds lovely."

"A thoroughly lovely day," Jessie agreed, wriggling out of her peach gown and throwing it on a chair.

"Are you seeing him again tonight?"

"No, the weekend at Lonsmere is still on. Simon thought it would do my career some good to know the high and mighty. You never know who'll turn up at these weekend parties, he says. But he's calling me next time he's in town."

"You'd better hurry. The minute bell just went," Tillie said, and walked quickly from the room, her hands clenched into fists.

It was another brilliant performance. Jessica was ecstatic, her mood enveloping the others on the stage and, eventually, the audience. Tillie had a fifteen-minute stretch when she was off; she sneaked up to the back of the balcony to watch. Jessie looked like an enchanted being, her gold hair a cloud around her face. Her figure was perfect, the fashion magazines notwithstanding. There was a restive stirring in the male portion of the audience every time she moved. No wonder Simon had switched his feeble affection to her. Who wouldn't? And she was extremely available into the bargain. No quibbling about first dates for Jessica Miter.

"If you say no on the first date, there's so often not a second one," she had once said bluntly. At least she wasn't a hypocrite about it.

Ron Beccles, in a fit of indiscretion, once told Jessie she was advancing her career faster on her back than most people could on their two feet. It was crude and vulgar, but true. As much as one disapproved of her, it wasn't really possible to dislike Jessie, either. She *was* warm, even with women. With men, Tillie imagined she was probably torrid. With a Simon Cranston, she would be instantaneous combustion.

After the show and the curtain calls, Jessie flew around the dressing room picking up bits and pieces to stuff into her overnight bag for the weekend at Lonsmere. What a whirlwind, exciting time she had. It didn't seem fair she should be rewarded for her immoral exploits in this way. Tillie wiped the makeup from her cheeks and carefully around the eyes, then went down the hall to see if the gang was going to Nick's.

"Coming along?" Ron asked.

"Sure. Why not?"

Saturday was a night that deserved better than going home alone—a night especially made for parties, dates, excitement. She looked to the dark corner where Simon's car had been parked the night before, and saw only gloomy shadows. The conversation in the group—all members of Gus's troupe—was invariably about the theater. They discussed not only their own plays but what was going on in London, on TV and in the movies. What they would do in the autumn was also a matter for discussion. If Gus made enough money, he would put on another set of plays next summer. If he didn't, there was some talk of taking the shows on the road, touring the provinces. They discussed the pros and cons of one-night stands in small towns, but really they all hoped Gus would take them on tour. The greasepaint was in their blood like an infection, raising their temperatures and their hopes and aspirations to a fever pitch.

Ron and another of the fellows shared a flat. They suggested the party adjourn there, to enjoy their ales at a cheaper price.

"I'm going home. I'm beat," Tillie said.

"Want to go to the beach tomorrow?" Ron called after her. It wasn't exactly a request for a date. The bunch hung around together.

"Maybe. I'll let you know."

She waved and went out into the street. It wasn't deserted yet, as it was Saturday night, but Brighton was small enough so that it wasn't bustling, either—as London or another large city would be. The smell of the sea was heavy on the air; the wind was blowing up from the south, turning quite cool.

She quickened her footsteps to her apartment and ran up the stairs, young enough to have this last burst of energy at the end of a long day. The phone was ringing when she got to her door. She fumbled with the key, wondering who it could be. A call so late at night invariably raised a fear in her mind. *Mom is sick!* was always what she thought, though her mother was a healthy, middle-aged matron involved in nothing more perilous than keeping house for her husband and one son still at home.

She hurried to the phone, her hand trembling as she lifted the receiver.

"Well, young lady, it's about time you got home," a low voice scolded. "Burning the candle at both ends, I see. I've been calling you since ten thirty. You'd better have a good excuse." It was Simon, talking as naturally as if . . . as if he hadn't spent the entire day with Jessica. "Well, what's your excuse?" he demanded in a playfully stern way.

"No excuse. I just got home from a date," she said, using the word loosely.

"I see. Here I have sat home like a lovesick boy, calling you every half hour, while you run around town with . . . *whom,* if I may make so bold as to ask?"

"Nobody you'd know."

"I detect a chill across the wires. My left ear is developing frostbite, while my thermometer reads seventy degrees. What can account for it?"

"Was there something in particular you wanted to discuss, Simon? I'm rather tired."

"You shouldn't stay out so late. What I wanted to know, but am rapidly becoming afraid to ask, was whether I could see you tomorrow. I thought I might run down to Brighton. Take a look at the waves, drop in and say hello to Lord Nelson and his fleet of lobsters. . . ."

Her heart gave a lurch. It sounded like a perfect day. But then there would be the evening, and it would be their second date, and he had been with Jessie all afternoon. "Don't I rate the London treatment?" she asked stiffly.

"Jessie has been bragging. Dare I hope that is jealousy I detect, flourishing in all its greenness amid the icicles?"

"Don't be silly. Of course I'm not jealous. We're only friends—acquaintances is more like it."

"Definitely icicles. Possibly even a touch of perma-frost. Just wait till I switch to my unfrozen ear, will you? There, that's better. Well, the reason I took Jessie to London, you see, is that she begged me to. I looked for you before the interview, but they told me you were late for work. A man has to eat, so I asked Jessie to join me for a quick bite before I returned to London. She had also expressed some intention of collapsing from starvation. It seemed the gentlemanly thing to ask her along. She was dying to see London. I didn't like to take her when I had to put her on a bus to go home, and more particularly when I wanted to eat before driving all the way to London. She bulldozed me into it. Comforted me with an apple she had in her purse. Actually I only got two bites. I had to do an interview in the afternoon with a couple of actors for their new movie, and she was burning to meet them, so she tagged along. I don't believe I alone was inducement enough for her to bus it back. Do you mind that I took her?"

"Of course not!"

"Too bad. I had hopes you'd be jealous."

"Don't be silly," she said, relieved at the explana-tion. It was just like Jessie to thrust herself on a celebrity, and then to make it sound as though it were a big affair. "We have no strings on each other."

"Speak for yourself. I'm trussed up like Gulliver on the beach."

"Idiot!" she said, relaxing into a laugh.

"That's more like it. I wish I were there to see that smile. Shall I pop into my Bentley and scoot down? It's only midnight—"

"No! No. Come tomorrow."

"Maybe that would be better. I have some work to

do. Write up Monday's column before I forget the brilliant aphorisms I invented for the actors' interview. Then I can relax tomorrow and enjoy the sun. And you. Do you own a bikini?"

"Does Texas have oil?"

"That's what I hear."

"I have a black, a white and a hot pink."

"What a mind-bending decision. Which is the smallest?"

"The black."

"Good. Wear it. We'll find a very quiet stretch of beach and scandalize the seagulls. I'll be there around two. Okay?"

"Fine. That means I can sleep in."

"Heavy date, I take it?"

"About a hundred and eighty pounds, but all muscle," she said to annoy him.

"Hmmm. Maybe I'd better go down tonight. You *are* alone, Ms. Brennan?"

"Oh yes, I didn't invite him up for coffee."

"That's my girl. I don't want you brewing up coffee with anyone but me. See you tomorrow."

"Right. Bye."

"Sleep tight."

She hung up the phone with a pensive smile on her face. He hadn't forgotten her, despite an afternoon of Jessie's warmer company. Maybe he liked her after all. He was interested enough, at least, to be making another trip to Brighton just to see her. They'd have a day at the beach together. She knew just the private spot she would take him to. It was a few miles down the coast, but Simon had a car—what a car! Who could tell what might happen, with the warm sun and the private beach and Simon, and her in her black bikini that Gus had called the most imaginatively immoral thing he had ever seen, and the most delightful. It kept her very happily awake, thinking about it. She'd have to phone Ron and let him know she wouldn't be going with the gang. She felt sorry for every woman in the troupe who wasn't her.

Chapter Four

Tillie knew as soon as she opened her eyes to the lead-gray skies next morning that there would be no afternoon at the beach. She feared Simon would not come at all, and kept casting fearful glances at the telephone. It didn't ring, indicating the date was still on. What on earth would they do if it rained? Her apartment was small and unstylish, an unlikely spot to entertain Simon, who must be accustomed to vast expanses of suede and chrome. She hardly knew how to dress, but because of the nip in the air, she selected a long-sleeved white silk blouse and a beige wraparound skirt that could pass for casual, or if he had something else in mind, could be dressed up with some jewelry and high heels.

"Hi. Nice day for ducks," he said when he came in at the appointed time.

"Oh, is it raining?" she asked, disappointed.

"Not yet, but it's no weather for mad dogs and Englishmen, either—not a drop of the noonday sun. Nice," he added, running a practiced eye over her outfit.

He looked better than nice himself. A beige cashmere jacket hung open to reveal a dark brown shirt open at the neck, and tan slacks.

"In fact, you rate the London treatment. I can't promise a clutch of actors, but if you'll settle for little old me, we can take the tourist's circuit of London: Saint Paul's, the Tower, Westminster Abbey. . . ."

"I'm not a total stranger to London. I've seen the architectural wonders."

"We could immerse ourselves in culture: art gallery, museum . . . nice and dry. Very dry," he added with a grimace.

"Would you like some coffee while we discuss it?" she asked—with a blush to remember the scarlet overtones a simple cup of coffee had assumed in their relationship.

He lifted a black brow at her as a slow smile stretched to a grin. "Black, please. It can't possibly replace the black bikini, but at least it will keep us awake till we come to some decision."

"There are some newspapers there, if you want to have a look at them while I make the coffee."

"I'd rather look at *you,* if you don't object to having me in the kitchen. I didn't come down from London to read the newspapers, after all."

He followed her into the cramped room, but was obliged to stay in the doorway, as two could not crowd into the space. He watched while she filled the pot, measured the coffee, set it to perk.

Simon talked the greatest foolishness while they waited for the coffee. He described the interview with the two actors, who were at loggerheads over billing for their new movie but determined to convince the world they were great friends and admirers of each other's work. "Actually, each is so fond of himself that neither of them even noticed I was accompanied by a fair-looking specimen of womanhood. Jess had to make do with the ogling of an octogenarian in the corner. I should have told her the fellow is a duke."

"That would not have impressed her nearly so much as a couple of actors. Nor me either," she added candidly.

Again he followed her to the kitchen for cups and saucers when the coffee was ready, offering to help by getting in her way, breaking crockery, spilling cream or sugar, or any other little service he could render.

"No, thanks. I can make a mess all by myself," she assured him. It was enervating to know those dark eyes followed her every movement.

"If you can't stand the chill, get out of the kitchen, I always say."

"Harry S. Truman," she answered quickly. "And it was the heat, not the chill."

"Why don't you show me your collection of books on trivia," he suggested. "Or your etchings, if you prefer."

"Why don't we decide where we're going, instead? The clouds aren't passing, but it's not raining either. Have you ever been to the Royal Pavilion?"

"I've managed to avoid it so far. Looks like my time is up. Actually, I'd like to see it. It might make an interesting item for my show one evening. Since I plan to spend a lot of time in Brighton this summer, I might as well start finding some material that will give me a legitimate excuse to be here. That way I can deduct the high cost of drinking your free coffee. Very good, by the way."

"Thank you."

"Did you know coffee has been drunk for over thirteen hundred years?"

"I didn't know that. Tea is even older, I believe."

"I've never done a show on tea. It is coffee we are discussing, to allow me to show off my trivia and my trip to Brazil." He described the cultivation, harvesting and blending of coffee, all in an amusing way, till they were ready to leave.

"Shall we go now?" she asked, picking up the cups.

"Very soon. Don't you think I've earned one little kiss, after all that history lesson on coffee? The Pavilion will be jammed with tourists. Gather ye coffee buds while ye may," he said, pulling her into his arms.

Tillie discovered that luxurious lobster-and-champagne nights had had nothing to do with the heady magic of being in Simon's arms. Her head spun as giddily as before, her blood rose as high. "Could we make that *two* little kisses?" he asked when at last she withdrew.

"I think we should go," she said with no conviction. She made no demur when he sat on the sofa with an arm around her, pulling her down with him.

"Your lips tell me no, but your eyes are giving them a hard argument. The eyes have it."

He lowered his head and kissed her again, more passionately, lounging on the sofa with his body pressing against hers. He slid his hands under her silk shirt, running his fingers lightly over her smooth skin with a gentle flutter, like butterfly wings. Her quivering response intensified to a golden glow with the increasing demands made by those exploring fingers. The radiance within threatened to bedazzle her common sense.

His lips slid across her cheek to her ear, leaving a trail of heat and causing a strange constriction in her chest. "I don't see why a girl who calls herself Ms. is wearing a brassiere," he murmured, opening the fasteners with suspicious ease. His touch was warm, intimate, on her sensitive skin—and deeply disturbing. A faint, shuddering sigh escaped her lips, then his lips were there to silence it. She placed her hands around his neck, feeling the tension in his muscles and the silky texture of his hair when her fingers curled through it. She was consumed with the need to be closer to him, to become a part of him, and she opened her lips to his, kissing him hotly, eagerly. She was immediately crushed in his arms, his hands sliding around her, molding her tightly against his body. The increasing fervor of his embrace and her own was arousing them both to a dangerous pitch.

Slowly, reluctantly, Simon released her. "Are you sure you want to see the Pavilion today?" he asked, his voice thick, his eyes smoldering.

The last thing she wanted to do was leave this enchanted spot, but there was still considerable doubt as to the seriousness of Simon's interest in her. "Desperately," she assured him, smiling at his scowl. "Did you know the stables at the Pavilion have an eighty-foot cupola sixty-five feet high, and there is a fountain in the middle to water the horses?"

"Good. I shall duck in for a quick shower. *Cold* shower," he added, rising to his feet and pulling her up after him. "But after the Pavilion and our lobster feast, dear heart, we shall return here for coffee."

She didn't know whether it was a promise or a threat, but knew the wise thing to do was to leave now while he was still on his feet, for his eyes kept returning to the sofa.

There were many tourists viewing the spectacular building erected by the Prince of Wales. Its white

onion domes, topped with gilt ornaments and surrounded by gardens, were among the chief attractions
of the city. They roamed from apartment to apartment, finding each more lavish than the last. Lotus
flowers and chandeliers; porphyry columns; low ori-
ental sofas with lion claws; mirrors and lights—it was
a sideshow of extravagant and bizarre taste. One
could only wonder at the man who devised such a
home.

"What could have induced him to such extrava-
gance?" Tillie mused.

"A woman, what else?" Simon replied. "This was
his love nest for his first wife, or whatever she was."

"Is there some doubt about it?"

"Apparently, as he married another lady without
legally divesting himself of Mrs. Fitzherbert. Yes,
there is certainly a good program here, and timely,
too."

"Timely? The man has been dead since the early
eighteen hundreds."

"Yes, but his crime lives on, and I don't refer to this
ghastly edifice."

"What *do* you mean, then?"

"Political corruption. What do you figure this place
cost to build back then?"

"Millions of pounds," she said, gazing at the finery.

"Precisely. Every penny of it gouged out of the
taxpayers, by various ruses. I don't know what your
sentiments on the matter may be, but when the
government takes *my* money—and they take plenty—
I like to know where it's going. Schools, hospitals,
medical help, looking after the aged or afflicted—that
I don't mind, but when I hear of large quantities going
into private coffers, my hackles rise."

"You are in a better position than most to do
something about it. Why don't you do a show on it?"

"There is a thing called slander, and another called libel. You have to have hard facts to back up such charges as that. It is a cliché that people get the government they deserve. I wonder if the good folks in the days of the Prince of Wales, later George the Fourth, really deserved him. I suspect a poor system of communications was the major crime."

"We have better communications now, with TV especially."

"That's right, and if we don't do something about political corruption, then we *do* deserve to be fleeced. There, I'm ready for that cold shower we spoke of. I get very hot under the collar when I take to riding my hobbyhorse. That, more or less, is the theme of the book I spoke to you about. Political corruption, government red tape, mismanagement of public funds. It's not easy to dig up facts. The culprits are in an unholy alliance. Like the tango, it takes two to execute bribery effectively. The giver is as guilty as the taker. You have to catch them with the dough in their hot little hands."

"A pity one of these crooks never offered *you* a bribe, Simon. Then you'd have him."

"My sentiments in the matter are too well known to make that likely. But I'm working on it. Never fear, Simple Simon is on guard."

They went on, looking at the elaborate kitchen and the stable with room for more than forty horses. "All this at a time when there were children starving in the gutter," Simon said, sneering at the place. "And this was only his holiday resort, you know. His real home was in London, at Carlton House. No wonder he was pelted with garbage in the streets."

"Was he really? What a shocking scandal."

"Your store of trivia has an empty shelf, woman. I should have thought you would know about Prinny.

His first public misalliance was with an actress. But then that breed has always been fair game—present company excepted, it goes without saying. But I shall say it anyway, to be on the safe side."

"I don't consider myself an actress. I mean to direct eventually," she reminded him. "Maybe even write a play when I'm older and have more experience."

"Quite the Renaissance woman, aren't you? You'll have to grow old on your own steam, but I'll be happy to help you with the experience."

"You already have. It's broadening talking to you."

"Thank you, but that is not the sort of experience I refer to."

After the tour, Simon went to speak to the manager about bringing a crew down to do some filming, and was directed to sources for background material. Tillie remained quietly on the sidelines, envying Simon his interesting job. He was made welcome, the red carpet rolled out for him, every help offered as though it was an honor. No wonder he was so broad in his interests. He had the ideal job, really—getting paid for learning all about the world around him. He was jetted in style to any corner of the globe that intrigued him. It was strange he should speak of another career, but then he probably wouldn't ever really write his book. Everyone had a dream, as she had the dream of writing plays. In the theater, they said every comedian wanted to play Hamlet, and every tragedian wanted to do farce.

She was pressed into service as a secretary, taking names of books and other information sources for the infamous Prince of Wales. Lord this and Lady that were mentioned. "Yes, I know him," Simon would say nonchalantly. "He'll certainly be cooperative. I did a show on his noble heap a year ago."

"Lady Morvane? I didn't know she was related to

the German nobility," he said, "though she *did* have a fine collection of Prussian antiques, now you mention it."

He had been everywhere and done everything. He certainly could be a help to her in the line of experience—legitimate learning experience.

It was getting late by the time they left. "Ready for dinner?" he asked.

"I have been dreaming of lobsters the past quarter of an hour."

"Would you mind terribly if I gave you a rain check on the lobster? I just remembered—that is, I am feeling—the need for red meat. A steak would go well, don't you think?"

"That suits me fine. I don't know just what place to recommend." Hamburgers were her normal fare when eating out.

"There's a good place toward Eastbourne, but not nearly that far. The Beefeater, it's called. It was highly recommended by a friend."

"I've heard of it," Tillie said, wondering if Jessie was the friend who had recommended it. It was Charles's favorite place.

They drove out of the city, along the coast, observing the sky and deciding wisely that the clouds were dissipating. "'Red sky at night, a sailor's delight.' Tomorrow the day will be fine—when I have to work and can't come to visit your bikini," he said. "I'll be making a few trips soon, though, to do the prince's pavilion. While I think of it, can I reserve next Sunday? Your having to work every night till ten thirty is going to cut into our gallivanting."

"I'm free next Sunday. I should go home to see Mom one of these weekends."

"I'll take you. Where does she live?"

"New York," she said, sliding a glance at him.

"That'll teach you to make rash promises. Actually, she lives in Kent, near Maidstone."

"Not to worry. I would have taken you to New York. You'll find I don't welsh on my promises, even the rash ones. Of course we would have had to hang around to do a few segments on the city's sights, but you wouldn't mind strolling through the subway with me, would you? Or we could film you having your purse snatched in Central Park. The alternatives are endless."

"It sounds charming. I'll see if I can talk my mother into moving."

"It's not absolutely necessary that a mother be the excuse for the trip," he said casually.

There were the inevitable curious people who recognized Simon when they entered the restaurant. Heads turned, but in this sophisticated spot, they limited their curiosity to stretching their necks. No one pushed an autograph book at him. They were taken to a corner table with a view of the sea—a nice, private spot.

"Could we sit over there?" Simon asked, pointing to another location. "The sun will soon be setting, and the light will be blinding," he explained to Tillie. There were curtains at the window, but they were an open, loose weave.

The table he chose was larger, for four, but the place was empty enough so that the waiter didn't object to the change. She thought Simon wasn't the sort who would take a refusal easily. He'd palm a folded bill into the man's hand, and that would be that.

"Cocktail?" he asked. "Or would you rather have wine? One feels at a place called the Beefeater, one should be ordering gin, but I shall have a red wine."

"I'll have the same. You choose."

"What do you recommend?" he asked the waiter.

A good dry Médoc was brought. They sipped it while scanning the menu and making their selections. "I'm not trying to strong-arm you, but the chateaubriand here enjoys a certain fame," he mentioned. "Of course, it must be shared by two. It isn't prepared for only one."

"By all means, let us have the chateaubriand. Did you know it was named after a French ambassador to England?"

"Certainly I did. The Vicomte François, you refer to?"

"Very likely," she said, dismayed at his knowing more about it than she did.

"The dish is good enough that I, for one, forgive him his horrible, unreadable novels. Don't pout, child. I'm older than you; furthermore, I did a program on foods named after famous people two years ago. I thought you were one of my faithful audience."

"That's probably where I learned that piece of trivia. And the Nesselrode who is responsible for the delicious pie was a Russian soldier or something, wasn't he?"

They discussed the Melba of peach Melba, pondered the Benedict of eggs Benedict, the Duke of Wellington of beef Wellington, and other gustatory delights. "I mean to enter the annals of food, too, one day," he told her. "Two lovers will be sitting here reading the menu a hundred years hence, wondering who was the Simon whose name they are reading."

"That will be a pie you have named in your honor, I assume? It was a pie man that Simple Simon stopped en route to the fair, you remember."

It was another perfectly enjoyable meal, with Simon's talk always interesting. Every item on the table and bit of antiquity on the restaurant's walls reminded him of an anecdote, usually related to his work. Many of the shows she remembered seeing. She had never dreamed in those days she would ever be having dinner with Simon himself.

They lingered over coffee. When it was done, and Tillie suggested they leave, Simon was reluctant. "Why don't we top it off with a liqueur?" he said.

Tillie didn't much care for liqueurs, they were so strong, but he recommended one "named after my Aunt Marie," which he said with a smile. The Tia Maria was sweet and delicious. She noticed that Simon glanced often toward the doorway as they sipped and talked.

"That's your friend, isn't it?" he asked suddenly.

She turned around to see Jessie enter with a gentleman that logic told her must be Charles Greville. She noticed that Charles was tall and austerely thin, with dark hair that had begun receding from his brow but had not yet gone far enough back to ruin his looks. He had the haughty looks associated with aristocracy: a long, pencil-thin nose; thin lips, not smiling; head held high. There was an air of dissipation about his face, mostly visible in the bleary eyes and pale complexion. He wore a navy blazer with a crest, and an ascot tucked into the front of his shirt. His ensemble looked incomplete without a captain's cap. The word *show-off* darted into Tillie's head, quickly followed by the realization that he was much too old for Jessie. He must be fifty, she thought.

Jessica made a suitably stupendous mate for the man. The speed with which her body had turned a golden brown in summer hinted that her natural complexion was brunette. This did not in the least detract from her beauty, however. Her bleached white hair hung in careful tangles past her shoulders.

She set off her dramatic coloring on this occasion by a black sun dress—chosen, no doubt, to give her a touch of sophistication.

There was nothing sophisticated in her greeting. She waved to them, smiled, shouted till everyone was looking at her; then she hastened toward their table. It was a grand entrance, Jessie's specialty. Damn, Tillie thought, the perfect day ending with this unwelcome company. She thought Simon would be as displeased as she to have their privacy invaded. Glancing at him, she saw she was mistaken. He was not only already on his feet but actually going forward to meet Jessie and her escort.

"Fancy meeting *you* here, as they say in the song," he said. "I don't have to ask if you enjoyed your day at Lonsmere. I can see you are positively glowing with joy."

"Super," Jessie cooed. "So you did come after all. Did you try the chateaubriand?"

"We did, and it was as good as you promised," he answered, looking expectantly to Charles, obviously waiting for an introduction.

Jessie presented her friend to them both. "Why don't you join us for a drink?" Simon asked.

Charles didn't look particularly eager. It was Jessie who said, "Lovely! We'd adore it, wouldn't we, Charles?"

Charles obediently took his seat, too well-bred to show his annoyance.

"What are you having?" Jessie asked, peering into Simon's glass. "It looks ghastly. May I try a taste?"

She took up his glass and sipped ever so daintily. "It's nice, but I'll have a sherry. Dry."

The house party had gotten to her. Jessie hated sherry, but if it was the drink served in the homes of the nobility, she'd drink it if it killed her.

She was a natural-born flirt. She probably didn't mean to offend anyone, but once she sat down at the table, all the masculine attention was hers. Tillie sat listening silently while Jessie regaled them with details of her weekend, every moment of which was spent in company with lords—trying to defend herself from their advances, to judge by her tone. When she stopped to sip her sherry, Simon turned to Charles.

"Lonsmere is near Chichester, isn't it?" he asked politely, to include Charles in the conversation.

"A few miles down the bay. Closer to the tip, actually," Charles deigned to reply.

"I visited it once, before your sister married Lord Travers."

"Oh really? Charming spot."

"It's beautiful. I did a show on Inigo Jones. The south portico is attributed to him, if memory serves. Of course it was added some years after the house was built."

"Right."

"Lady Travers is redoing the royal suite," Jessie interrupted. "All in red plush, with oodles of gilt and antiques and things."

"Not quite so garish as it sounds," Charles explained, smiling at her enthusiasm. "She was fortunate enough to get hold of the old family bedstead at Sotheby's, and is redoing the room in its original fashion."

"It's a heavy financial burden, keeping up the old and stately homes nowadays," Simon said. "Many of them are falling into the hands of the National Trust."

"Not *my* place," Charles said swiftly, defiantly. "My own home, Wespark, is nearby, Simon. Have you ever seen it? Old Tudor heap, rather pretty really, if you go for rose brick. Some interesting diapering work . . . gives us its date. Early sixteenth century."

"I've seen it from the road only."

"Falling apart inside, but I'm patching it up as best I can. Roof needs work. West wing is in some disrepair."

"He's shamming it," Jessie declared. "It's gorgeous, just like a palace, or the movies."

"Yes, a horror movie. Decaying splendor is the girl's idea of gorgeous. Not fit even to be opened to the public to make a few pounds from giving tours, as so many of them are doing."

"Is Lonsmere open to the public?" Simon asked.

"Yes, Tuesdays, Thursdays and, unfortunately, Sundays. The weekends are the best time for hauling in the shopgirls and typists," he added condescendingly. "Of course, the riffraff is not allowed in the family's private living quarters. They just go about ogling the state rooms."

"Lord Travers had a beautiful yacht in the water the day I was there," Simon continued, apparently interested in continuing in this vein. "Do you do any yachting? Your land runs down to the water as well, if I'm not mistaken?"

"I have a motor launch," Charles said. "Used to do some yachting when my father was alive. Demmed thing sprang a dozen leaks, and I traded it in on a little motor launch. That yacht was used to rescue our men from Dunkirk."

"The new launch is super," Jessie added, feeling Charles was not adept at bragging. "It sleeps four. Why, you've gone for all sorts of longish trips on the *Erin*," she reminded him.

"Not quite across the Atlantic," he explained. "You do any boating at all, Simon?"

"Sailing, not motoring. I have a yawl at Lyme Regis, near my home. I don't get much time for it. I once sailed to the Caribbean with friends. I find I prefer to travel by jet. It gets you where you're going faster, and leaves more time for sight-seeing. Sailing becomes rather boring after a while."

"That's true. Have you tried the Concorde yet?" Charles asked.

"I flew to the States the month it started making that route. Incredible—crossing the Atlantic in the time it used to take to drive a few hundred miles."

"I did the same. Where do you put up when you're in New York?" Charles asked. "The Waldorf is falling off in service, don't you think?"

"I prefer the newer places. The Hilton is always reliable."

"Unfortunately, one may meet anyone at a Hilton hotel," Charles pointed out. "I prefer the old, smaller places that restrict their clientele. No one wants to rub shoulders with rock stars and movie stars and *nouveau riche* oilmen from any country. A Ritz hotel is usually decent. Switzerland is the place that really knows how to run a hotel. Thank God Ritz exported the talent to other places. Do you know, even at very expensive new hotels, they don't pick your shoes up outside your door at night and have them back polished in the morning? Actually, I left mine outside one night and had them stolen. If they hope to cater to gentlemen, they ought to give the sort of service a gentleman is accustomed to."

"All the hotels are cutting back on the service," Simon agreed.

"Switzerland is still decent. I usually nip over during the Christmas break, when the house isn't sitting. Do a spot of skiing."

The "in" places for skiing were the next topic on the agenda. Jessica sat soaking it up like a sponge, her eyes sparkling with desire. Tillie, listening quietly, began to think the two men were engaged in a battle of one-upmanship, showing off their taste and experience. They went on from skiing to motor cars, tailors, clubs. The ways of spending large sums of money were endless. As sure as Simon proclaimed Brook Street tailors the best, Charles would dredge up some Roman tailor who made better jackets, or insist Pierre Cardin was the last man alive who could create a cravat. If Simon praised his Bentley, Charles had to prefer a Rolls, or sigh after a Clenet or Excalibur. When Charles proclaimed Maxim's the best eatery in all of France, Simon insisted his last meal there had been unsatisfactory.

Tillie had no way of knowing if this conversation was typical of Charles, but she knew very well it was not the way Simon usually spoke to her. He was putting on an exhibition to impress Charles Greville, member of parliament, possessor of an old family name and mansion. It was social climbing of the most blatant sort, and she was disgusted with him.

"We must get together one of these weekends, the four of us, and do something," Charles was soon suggesting. "Why don't we take the ladies to Paris?" he said.

Jessie squealed and clapped her hands.

"You forget we have a play on Saturday night," Tillie reminded her. "There's not much point going on Sunday just for one day. Everything would be closed."

"That's true. We could go after we close in August, though. We'll have a week or so off then. Is it a date?" Jessie asked, wanting to get it settled.

"I don't like to make dates so far in advance," Tillie said, with very little interest in the scheme.

"I don't know that far ahead where I'll be either, or

what I'll be doing," Simon agreed. "But it doesn't have to be Paris, surely. We'll think about it, and do something here, or in London."

He had already asked her out for next Sunday, but if he thought she was going to put up with a whole day of his vying with Charles for who could spend the most money, he was mistaken. She could hardly say so in front of the others, so instead she suggested it was time they be getting home.

"It's early," Simon said, looking at his watch.

"Ah, a Cartier. Very nice," Charles said, lifting his own wrist to flaunt his Patek Philippe.

"I always liked my Timex," Tillie said, brandishing her cheap timepiece. Jessie gave her a repressive stare, but some demon possessed her. She wanted to show the men she was not taken in by their ranting. Money did not equal class, especially when it was interminably boasted of. "I got it at the five-and-ten, where I buy my lingerie. Most of my things are from the same shop. I like things to match."

Charles looked across the restaurant, ignoring her. Jessie said quickly, to cover this awful gaffe, "Harrods has a sale on."

"Yes, but the bus service is so inconvenient, isn't it?" Tillie pointed out. "And the train is awfully expensive. But then I don't usually nip over to Rome or New York for a weekend, and these things do well enough for the fish-and-chips hut."

"Tillie is such a joker," Jessie explained, smiling.

"We'll improve her style," Simon said, but not in an amused way. He was unhappy with her.

"I didn't know you found my style so objectionable, Simon," she replied, her tone snippy. "Well, are you two through comparing jets and yachts and tailors? Shall we go now? I don't know about you plutocrats, but I have to get up early and walk to work tomorrow. And you, Simon, have to cruise your Bentley back to your suede-and-chrome apartment, no doubt to be parked by the doorman."

"The doorman holds the door, darling," Jessie said, exasperated.

"Oh really? I thought his job was only decorative. They do look so amusing dressed up like Austrian generals, don't they?"

"It is getting a little late," Simon said, but with no sign of appreciating her sarcasm.

They all arose to leave. "My place is only a few miles down the road, if you'd like to come out for a nightcap," Charles suggested.

"Sounds like a good idea," Simon answered, angering Tillie even more.

"Not for me, thanks," she said swiftly. "You can drop me off at my place, Simon."

"Fine. I'll do that, and meet you at Wespark, Charles," he said.

She could hardly believe her ears. She sat as silent as a jug in the car as he took her home. "Sure you won't change your mind?" he asked as they approached her apartment. "It's only ten o'clock."

"Quite sure, thank you."

"Why not?"

"I didn't much care for the company."

"How many chances do you get to visit the homes of the old rich?"

"Not many. I manage to get along without that honor."

"I consider it more of a duty than an honor."

"Duty? It seemed to me you enjoyed showing off very much."

"There's a streak of the actor in all of us. I *did*

enjoy it, just as you enjoyed pushing your Timex in our faces and letting on you bought that well-tailored silk shirt in the five-and-ten. I cannot vouch for the lingerie, but your outer garments are of quality materials and workmanship."

"I still don't see what duty has to do with it."

"You said you wanted to write. Your experiences so far in your life have been somewhat limited, to judge by your conversation. This is a chance to meet a different type of person. A broadening experience for you."

She made an indistinguishable "hmphing" sound, and again fell silent. She had some heavy thinking to do. "Good night. Thanks for the dinner and the tour of the Pavilion. They were both very nice," she said when the car stopped at her door.

"You're welcome. I enjoyed them too. I'll give you a call later in the week, okay?"

"Sure," she said, reaching for the door handle, as he made no move of doing it for her.

"Are you in that big a hurry?" he asked.

"I wouldn't want you to keep Charles and Jessie waiting. They might start on the champagne without you. I'm sure it's champagne that will be served, probably Dom Perignon, in golden goblets."

"I have him pegged for a brandy man. Courvoisier. I'll let you know which of us is right." He opened his door and got out, went to open hers, and took her fingers in his as they walked toward her door.

"Can I take a rain check on my coffee?" he asked. "You *did* promise I could come back after dinner for coffee."

"It wasn't an open invitation, Simon. I'm not running a restaurant here, in case you've gotten that idea."

"No Swiss blood in you. That's the trouble. They run a much more gracious hostelry."

"No blue blood in me either, to compensate for it."

"It is an unforgivable cliché I know, but you're so pretty when you're angry," he said, bending to kiss her nose. With a light laugh, he turned and ran back to his car. *Ran!* He actually couldn't wait to get out to Wespark, back to the high-born braggart and Jessie.

She wondered just which of them was the main attraction. She knew at least it was Jessie's idea that they go to the Beefeater. Was that why he had lingered so long over coffee—why he had suggested a liqueur—to have an excuse to wait till she came? But really it was mainly Charles he had tried to ingratiate. If he wanted to be with Jessie, he could have asked her out today. She would have gone in a flash and made some excuse to Charles.

Was he using Jessie to smooth his path to Charles? He liked to speak of the famous people he knew. To be an intimate friend of a well-known member of parliament would flatter his ego. He knew many actors, movie stars, writers and so on, but how many upper-class, old-rich people was he on close terms with? When he went to their estates, it was as an interviewer, not a friend. Was that it? Was he an ordinary garden-variety snob and social climber?

She was very dissatisfied with the ending of their date. For whatever reason, he preferred to be with Charles and Jessica to being with her, and that was hard to accept. She liked him more than he liked her. She rejected the word "love" that clamored for recognition. She would have passed up an invitation to Buckingham Palace for another hour alone with him, but that obviously wasn't *his* feeling. She was only a diversion, a pleasant way to pass a Sunday afternoon when he had nothing more exciting to do. Would he even have bothered with that, if he hadn't had some plans laid to meet Jessie and Charles afterward at the Beefeater? That was why he hadn't wanted to go to the Nelson spot for lobster. He'd arranged the meeting in advance.

Chapter Five

Monday brought another unpleasant surprise. Jessie wafted in fifteen minutes late for rehearsal of *The Rivals*.

"Sorry, Tillie. I was so darned late last night, I slept till noon. And I had to sunbathe an hour before I came. My tan fades so fast, you know."

"Late night with Charles?" Tillie asked.

"No, with Simon. We only stayed half an hour, then he offered to drive me home, to save Charles the bother. He stayed till all hours. I couldn't get rid of him—what a guy! But I don't mind. It was a good opportunity for me to discover who's who at the BBC. I mean, if you don't know someone, you haven't got a chance of landing a job. He said they're casting a new sitcom for next January, and looking for a luscious blonde who looks good in a bikini, so next time he's in town, I'm going to model for him."

"How charming."

"He'll be in Brighton on Wednesday to talk to the people at the Royal Pavilion. He's doing a show on it."

"Yes, I know."

"I hope he calls me. You had a date with him yesterday, he tells me."

"Yes, we went out for dinner."

"I never said you could have Simon, you know. It was Charles I suggested you go out with. How did Simon come to call *you?*"

"Why, I imagine it was only because you were busy, Jessie," Tillie answered, her tone ironic.

"That's probably it," Jessie decided, accepting her answer at face value. "When I told him we would probably stop off at the Beefeater on our way home from Lonsmere, I didn't expect *you* to be with him."

"Sorry if I got in your way."

"Oh, you didn't. Actually, I was glad Simon was with a girl, so Charles wouldn't get too suspicious. I'm not through with him yet. He's going to introduce me to a fellow who does portraits of famous people. We're hoping he'll offer to do one of me. Wouldn't it be super?"

"What would you want that for?"

"Are you kidding? He's having a big exhibition in September. There I'd be, hanging side by side with prime ministers, maybe even the royal family. Everybody would see me. He doesn't do anybody but celebrities. Something would be bound to come of it."

"You're incorrigible, Jessie."

"In this business, you have to be if you want to get anywhere. Shall we get on with this rehearsal? I want to get to the beach before the sun disappears."

The rehearsal went on, allowing Tillie's mind a rest from thinking about Simon. She could still lose herself in her work, deciding what gestures the actors should adopt; what speeches were to be emphasized; correcting movement and stage placement of the actors; and mostly trying to tame Jessie's flamboyant presentation of Lydia Languish. It was engrossing, interesting, and great fun. It was only when the stage was cleared and the work over that her mind reverted to *him*. She made a determined effort to forget Simon. She even skipped his nightly show and went out with Ron Beccles and the rest of the gang for a hamburger—instead of rushing to her apartment to watch it. Then it was back to the theater for the evening performance.

Tuesday passed in a similar manner. Simon had said he would phone. She was angry with herself for going straight home after the play, in case he did call. Jessie had said he was coming to Brighton on Wednesday. If he meant to see her, he'd call Tuesday. There was no call. She told herself she didn't care; that she was better off without him. He was a social climber, a rake—staying till all hours at Jessie's apartment. If he was dangling the plum of a role in a TV sitcom before her, he'd expect some payment for it—and the currency Jessie used with men was no secret.

When finally he called, it was seven o'clock on Wednesday evening. He called her at the theater. "Hi. I'm in town, phoning from the Pavilion, in fact. Can I see you tonight?"

"You know I have the show to do."

"I meant after the show. I'll stick around here, have a late dinner and meet you afterward. I'll probably catch the last act. The one where the audience learns what a conniving female you are."

She was too angry by then to accept. He phoned at the last minute, taking for granted she would be willing to drop any plans she had and run to him, just because he happened to be in town.

"Sorry, Simon. I already have a date," she lied airily.

"With the walking muscle?" he asked.

"Who else?"

"Hmmm, I don't think I like that."

"Did you expect me to sit on my thumbs waiting to see if you happened to call?"

"No, I expected you to offer to break the date. You can see Mr. Muscle anytime. Is he the fellow who plays the fiancé in the play?"

"That's right."

"Is this serious, between the two of you?"

"I'm serious about my career, at this particular time. Men have to take a back seat. Sorry. Why don't you call me next time you're in town? Or even *before* you come."

There was a longish pause from the other end. "See you Sunday," he said. "Bye." The receiver clicked, and the hum on the wire told her he had hung up. He sounded angry, she thought with satisfaction. She also remembered she had a date with him on Sunday, but she would say clearly she did not want to spend the day with Charles and Jessie. While these thoughts ran through her mind, the phone rang, startling her.

"Brighton Theater," she said.

"Can I speak to Jessie Miter, please?" a voice asked. It was Simon. He was going to ask Jessie out.

"I'll get her," she said angrily.

"Hey, is that *you?*" he asked loudly. She heard it distinctly, but pretended she had not. She called down the hall to Jessie.

"You'd better hurry. It's nearly curtain time," she said.

"Is it Charles?" Jessie asked.

"No, it's—I think it's Simon Cranston."

"Oh goodie!" she said, jiggling her shoulders.

"Hello, Simon darling," she cooed into the mouth-piece. Tillie turned and walked quickly from the room.

When Jessie returned to the dressing room, she was crowing about a date with Simon after the play. "We have to go somewhere that Charles won't find out," she said. "Simon doesn't want to make him jealous. Isn't he thoughtful? We're driving to Hove or Port Slade. They have dancing at the Port. It's farther, but in a Bentley, who cares?"

The performance was splendid that night, if a little faster-paced than quite suited a serious drama. Jessie was eager to get through with it so she could get on with her date. Tillie, wondering if Simon was in the audience for the third act, was nervous, fumbled a few lines and cursed herself. It was unprofessional behavior, unworthy of her.

Afterward, she went to Ron's dressing room, mostly to absent herself from Jessie's when Simon came backstage, as she imagined he would do. She waited ten minutes, using Ron's mirror and cream to remove her makeup while he changed into street clothes behind the screen.

"Are the kids going to the tavern tonight?" she asked.

"Yeah, are you coming along?"

"Sure, why not?" she answered listlessly. It would be better than going home alone to think about Simon and Jessie.

When they came out of his dressing room together, the door of the room she shared with Jessie was closed. "Can you wait a sec till I change? I just have to put on my slacks and a shirt."

"I'll tell the gang to go on. We'll meet them there."

Ron called to the passing troupe, who stopped for a little good-natured teasing before going on their way.

Tillie opened the door and found Jessie in Simon's arms, engaged in a passionate embrace. She felt a rush of blood to her head and a heavy thumping in her chest. Simon's head came up abruptly. He stared in dismay, first at Tillie, then over her shoulder at Ron.

For a minute, Tillie was frozen to the spot. She should say something, should close the door—anything. "Sorry. I didn't mean to intrude," she said.

"Oh, you're not! I'm just thanking darling Simon. He spoke to the casting director about me," Jessie said, smiling from ear to ear. "Isn't it super?"

"Wonderful. Congratulations," Tillie said, then closed the door quickly.

Ron looked at her and laughed. "Jessie never minds performing in public, but her friend looked fit to be tied. It's Simon Cranston, is it? The guy from TV?"

"Yes. I . . . I don't know what I should do. I have to get changed. I thought they'd be gone by now," she said, her words all coming out in a rush.

"We'll respectfully request they hand your clothes out the door. You can change in my room," Ron said, taking a step toward the closed door.

It opened before he reached it, and Simon's head came out. "You aren't interrupting anything. Come right in," he said, looking slightly pink about the collar.

"Sorry about that, sir," Ron said, smiling slyly.

"Sir?!" Simon exclaimed, looking with definite pique at the young man. He turned to Tillie. "Aren't you going to introduce me to your friend?" he asked.

She made the introduction stiffly, evading Simon's eyes as much as possible. When she glanced up, she noticed Simon was measuring Ron, assessing his appearance, perhaps even his muscles and probable weight.

"I'm ready, Simon," Jessie said, giving herself a

shot from the perfume atomizer on her table, always her last move before leaving the room. "I'm wearing Night of Love, a new scent," she said, thrusting her wrist under his nose. "Do you like it?"

"Appropriate," Ron muttered in a low aside.

Jessie looked ravishing as usual, this time in a navy and white close-fitting dress, with high-heeled back- less pumps to minimize her ankles. It was pleasing to know there was one flaw in that body. Her ankles were fleshy.

Simon leaned his head toward Tillie as he passed her at the doorway. "Not an ounce over one seventy- five," he said quietly, then left without looking back. They made a handsome couple, even from behind.

Tillie changed quickly, not noticing what she threw on. It hardly mattered, to go and sip beer in a dark pub with the group from the play. It was impossible not to wonder where Simon and Jessie were going— not very satisfying either, to know she could have been the one with Simon if she had wanted. If it made no difference to him, what was the point? She would not cheapen herself by running after him. She stayed at the pub till midnight, then walked home with Ron, who was going her way.

Next morning at eight, she was awakened by the phone shrilling in the living room. She leaped from her bed, checking her clock to see that she hadn't overslept. A call in daylight held no secret terrors. She didn't think of sickness, accident or death, but of some pest trying to sell her a newspaper or magazine subscription.

"Hello," she said irately.

"Good morning to you, too, Miss Sleepyhead," Simon said in a disgustingly cheerful voice.

"Oh, it's you. What do you want?" she asked, in about as rude a voice as she ever used to anyone.

"I wanted to report it *was* Courvoisier brandy Charles Greville serves his guests. Did we have a bet on it, by the by?"

"No, we didn't. Did you get me out of bed at eight o'clock to tell me that?"

"No. I understood a poor working girl like you struggled into her Woolworth's shirt at eight by her Timex watch. Sorry if I woke you. I really called to ask if you had a good time last night."

"Very good, thanks. And you?"

"Also good, considering."

"Considering what?"

"Considering I wasn't with you, dear heart, but more particularly considering I knew you were with another man. Were you showered with Night of Love too, before you left the room?"

"Of course I was."

"Good. That guarantees the Muscle couldn't have got too close to you. I wish Charles would give her some decent perfume."

"Don't be such a cheapskate. Buy her some yourself. Try Chanel Number Five."

"Charles wouldn't like Chanel. The shopgirls are wearing it nowadays. Patou he might accept."

"Yes, well, if you're through discussing Jessie's perfume, I think I'll run along now."

"Hold your horses. I have other details to discuss. I have to take a run out to the Pinewood movie studio this afternoon, and tomorrow I have a couple of Oxford dons coming into the studio to discuss slang and jargon and other linguistic barbarisms. Don't I have an exciting life? It looks as if we won't be able to get together before Saturday. If you tell me you have a date with the Muscle, I shall reach my hands down the telephone wires and squeeze the breath out of your lily-white neck. I'll be at the stage door at ten thirty. Be ready. And Tillie—"

"Now just a minute!"

"Wear something sexy. We're stepping out. Now you can go back to bed. Good-bye."

She slammed the phone down, then picked it up again to phone him and tell him she would certainly not be waiting for him on Saturday night. What made him think she had nothing else to do? She realized she didn't have his number, or know whether he was at home or work, or even have a London telephone directory in the apartment. She slammed the receiver down again, suddenly lighthearted, admitting to herself she was delighted she would be seeing him again soon.

The two of them would go out alone. She would tell him she didn't like Charles, and he would be sensitive enough to know she didn't like the way he acted in Charles' company. He would explain the reason for it. Just what the explanation could be she didn't know or try to imagine. Everything would be as it was before. And she *would* wear something sexy, too. Jessie wasn't the only one with a figure. Her own wasn't so full as Jessie's, but she was in better shape from a health point of view. Her ankles were trimmer too, she thought with satisfaction.

Saturday night was fine, but not at all the way Tillie anticipated. Simon brought a whole slew of people down from London with him, rented a private suite at The George, and threw a party. He came with a program director, a television actor, two producers and a fellow writer from the newspaper. The guests from Brighton included Gus Brooks and the actors from the stock company, along with Jessie and Tillie.

"Wasn't it *sweet* of Simon to do it?" Jessie sighed

blissfully as she slipped out of her costume at the end of the play. "I hinted to him a dozen times, but I didn't think he'd really do it. This could be a fantastic break for us all. It would take us *years* to come to the attention of so many influential people by ourselves. Funny he didn't bring the casting director with him— the one he spoke to about me. I expect one of the producers is the fellow who'll be producing the sitcom I'm after. I must find out which one he is and be nice to him. Oh, I *do* adore Simon. He could make me a star, if only I could convince him to do it."

"You don't have a date with Charles tonight?" Tillie asked.

"No, and Simon knew it too. I wonder if that's why he chose tonight to bring them. I happened to mention on the phone that Charles had to go up to London. Something to do with the government."

"Did Simon call you?" Tillie asked, instantly suspicious.

"Yes, to check on our double date tomorrow. You haven't forgotten, Tillie, have you? Remember, they wanted to take us to Paris, but since we have to work Saturday nights, we decided to meet here. Let's see if we can get them to take us to London."

"Yes, I'd forgotten, actually," Tillie said, trying to remain calm. She hadn't so much forgotten as hoped Jessie had done so.

"Simon wasn't at all keen on the London idea. Maybe he brought these people down from the BBC to placate me. We're to spend the day at Charles's place, Wespark. He's going to take us out on his motor launch. I suppose we'll go out somewhere for dinner, maybe London."

An entire day in the company of Charles and Jessie sounded like prolonged torture. Simon must have noticed she didn't like them. Why had he gone behind her back, phoned Jessie and arranged this disagreeable day for them?

But it was hard not to be infected with the enthusiasm that ran through the rest of the troupe that night. They were all excited about the opportunity of meeting VIPs from the BBC. The BBC could televise Gus's plays if they wanted to and make them all overnight celebrities. It was kind of Simon to have arranged the party, but if the kindness was done to appease Jessie, it was no compliment to her.

At least she had him to herself in the car on the way to the hotel. "What made you decide to do this, Simon?" she asked.

"Old times' sake. It would be nice if Gus could get another crack at the big time. His new play is pretty good, I think. It needs work, but these two weeks on the boards will have shown him that, if he's still as good as he used to be. A fellow likes to encourage the arts, and artists."

"Do you think they might do it on TV?"

"It's possible. I invited Ted Dorrit, the program director, along with that in mind. He's the one who selects what will be shown."

"Which fellow decides whether Jessie will be in the new sitcom you told her about?" she asked, trying to make it not sound catty.

"Ron Leduc. He should keep her out of our hair. I want you to meet Larry Moss. He's a bright new director. You might scrounge some help from him. Talk to him about your *Rivals*. I don't know that he's ever directed it, but he's bound to have seen it a dozen times, and might be of some help."

Tillie was ambitious enough to feel a fire glowing within her at the approaching party. It wasn't easy to get the ear of such people as Larry Moss, a name encountered thus far only on the TV screen.

"What's he like?" she asked.

"Ugly as sin. You didn't think I'd bring one of the handsome ones down to steal my girl away, did you?" he asked, smiling and reaching for her hand in the darkness. "The local competition is strong enough. Why didn't I think to find a part that would take Mr. Muscle away on location—far away."

Encouraged by this overture, she asked, "Why did you arrange for us to spend tomorrow with Jessie and Charles?"

"Necessity, my dear. I don't relish it any more than you do, but we'll escape them right after dinner."

"What necessity?" she persisted.

"A business necessity. Charles is one of the bright lights of the government. I could discover all sorts of things from him if I could work my way into his good books. It's hard to deal with politicians. Before they'll agree to come on a show, you have to promise you won't ask them anything of the least interest to the audience. They have to see the list of questions and approve them in advance so as to get their answers down pat. They want a platform to preach their doctrine, not a chance to be questioned on their performance. They have a very tight social circle, too; they stick together. It seems a good chance to find out what's going on in the inner sanctums of the house. Charles has been known to take a little more booze than is good for his discretion, you know."

"I see," she answered, mollified somewhat. A man's career had to come first, but she was sorry it had to come first on the few occasions she saw Simon.

"Tonight, I help you. Tomorrow, you help me. Okay?"

"I guess so."

He had certainly gone to a good deal of trouble and expense to help her and the rest of Gus's outfit. Food and drinks were awaiting them on a linen-covered table. Simon took her hand and introduced her to Larry Moss. He was as ugly as promised, a woolly sheep dog of a man with curly hair from the crown of his head to about three inches below his chin. A little pink face peeped out from amid the mounds of hair. He had bright brown eyes, a large nose and a bushy mustache.

"Hiding behind all that hair, there's a very clever director, Tillie," Simon said. "This is the woman I spoke to you about, Larry."

"You forgot to mention that she was gorgeous, my good man," Larry said, eyeing Tillie carefully.

"I knew you'd see it for yourself. I didn't want you shaving or seeing a barber before you came. Oh, and I forgot to tell *you* Larry is married," Simon said to her. "The father of three bouncing boys, and the husband of an extremely jealous wife . . . who happens to be a crack shot," he added, laughing.

"Should I have worn an armored vest?" Tillie asked.

"Certainly not. When you have a body like Venus, you cover it as lightly as the law allows," Larry told her, bowing formally. "Run along now, Simon. Tillie and I are going to fill two large glasses with Scotch, find a dark corner and discuss drama."

"Make mine a Pimm's," she countered.

With this one alteration in the plans, they did just as Larry had outlined. She found him a fascinating man, and forgot his ugliness as soon as he began to speak, both knowledgeably and interestingly about the theater. He had worked with many stars and had amusing stories about each, but of more interest to a budding director, he had *ideas*.

"In my experience," he said, "the major fault in today's directing is that the director wants to be the star. Fellini, Bergman, Renoir—all actors manqué. They would much prefer to be before the camera. A director's job is to direct. The word comes to us from the Germanic, and means a rudder. We directors must take that far step down to realize we are only the rudder steering the ship of the play. Realize, Tillie, that the actors are the stars, and they are your tools, as the printed pages of the play are your medium. With the tools the producer supplies you, you must hone the play into a creditable and enjoyable performance."

"But sometimes the tools don't seem quite right for the job, do they?" she asked, thinking of Jessica, her tool for Lydia Languish.

"Indeed they do not. One might be forgiven for suspecting that producers purposely give us a pair of tweezers when what we require is a large pair of pliers. Or a hammer when what we need is a needle. That's when it's good to remember you're a navigator, or rudder, if you prefer. Steer your course in the direction of the prevailing wind; that is, take into account your stars' abilities and disabilities. If you have a fine *under*-actor, and I confess they are my own favorite tools, then you can present a finely tuned, complex, subtle performance. If they stick you with a ranter, you sail your ship to his wind. Forget precision, forget complexity, hang up philosophy. Go for the emotions: the laugh, the tears. Olivier's *Richard III* is not Kean's *Richard III*. Now, I see—how can one help but notice her, even without looking?—they have handed you a blond sex symbol to play Lydia Languish. There is not a languishing atom in the girl's body. This will be a monumental challenge for you. It staggers the imagination to picture Jessica as a romantic ninny wanting to throw away the half of her fortune. You will, perforce, present a farcical play.

Realize that fact before you begin, or you will be faced with a resounding fiasco. *The Rivals* takes well to farce; the situation is not at all desperate. I wish you every luck."

"There, you have solved my problem in one speech," Tillie said, grateful for his advice.

"Experience has solved it. The young always want to be thought sophisticated. I cannot imagine why, when the major charm of youth is its innocent lack of sophistication. Be naïve with your play. Don't try to make it subtle, or to say anything about today's morality. No one but a moron goes to the theater to be instructed; one goes to enjoy himself, and there should be good enjoyment in your farce."

They talked long about her play, and about others. Tillie was so engrossed she forgot the people around her. For a full hour the two directors discussed the theater, or rather, Larry talked and she listened. She looked around the room occasionally, mostly to glance at Simon, but he was not paying more than a polite share of attention to Jessie—who was trying her wiles on the producer with very good success. What time she had left over she devoted to the one actor present. A face she saw regularly on the screen and in the tabloids was irresistible to Jessica.

"And now it is time you and I be polite, and speak to the other members of the party," Larry decided.

Tillie thanked him, then looked around for Simon. She discovered he was gone. Before long, she noticed that Jessie was also missing. Her curiosity soon raised itself to jealousy. They had obviously gone off together, just the two of them. She joined another group: a producer, Ron, and a few of the other actors from Gus's outfit. Her mind wandered out the door after Simon while people talked and drank and nibbled on food from trays.

She had another drink and sipped slowly. Her eyes often went to the door, but after thirty minutes, Simon and Jessica still hadn't returned. It was unforgivable of Simon to humiliate her like this. Without another word, she slipped quietly out the door and asked the doorman to get her a cab. She peeped her head in at the bar on the way out—and saw them. Simon and Jessie were at a table in a dark corner, their heads together, talking. She could not hear their words, but there was intimacy in their attitudes. They were completely engrossed in each other. They didn't even see her. She went home, locked the apartment door and turned out all the lights, in case he came there looking for her.

At twelve thirty, he still hadn't come. She got undressed and went to bed. She was no sooner under the sheets than the phone rang. It rang seven times, then stopped. No one came to the door. Simon had got up that party for Jessica. He was only using Tillie as an excuse, so Charles wouldn't be annoyed if he caught wind of any rumors linking Simon with Jessie. Simon didn't want to alienate precious Charles.

Chapter Six

Tillie was angry when she awoke on Sunday morning. She was angry enough to break the Sunday date with Simon, but he had been kind to Gus and the troupe. He had stayed overnight at The George for this date, and it would be too rude to break it, but she wouldn't make any other appointments to see him. If it was Jessie he was interested in, then he would have to find some other gullible female to be used to fool Charles. She wouldn't be unpleasant, or show him in any way how angry she was. She would be polite, even friendly, but she would protect her heart against further damage.

When Simon phoned at eleven, she did not say a word about having seen him with Jessie at the bar. "I got the most ripping headache last night," she explained calmly. "I'm terribly sorry I had to dash off without seeing you and thanking you, but I didn't see you around when I wanted to leave. I came straight home to bed."

"Headaches already, and we're not even married yet," he said, making a joke of it. "I figured that was it. I didn't worry, as Mr. Muscle was there till the cock crowed. I saw you deep in talk with Larry, so I stepped out for a minute. I had to make some phone calls, and went to my room."

"Larry was nice. He helped me a lot," she replied, pretending to believe his lie.

"He was impressed with you, too. He mentioned the eyes, as well as the brain. I think they're more stormy gray than charcoal, myself. Did he really help?"

"Immensely. Mostly with insights."

"Insights into your character, or your characters?"

"He cautioned me against trying to do a sophisticated play. I'm not totally sure what he meant, but I understood most of what he was saying."

"Ah well, that's better than most of us do. I have all kinds of news for you that came about after you left. Gus stuck around for an hour or so after the kids went home. The BBC is going to do his new play, and let him direct, but not with the present cast. I bucked for it, but was shot down. The cast are rank amateurs, when you come down to it. It will cancel the tour, but Gus plans to resume the school during the winter. We're trying to get the actors placed here and there—bit parts mostly, you know—but it will keep body and soul together, and give them a little experience. At least actors aren't like salaried employees; they are accustomed to batting around from pillar to post."

"That's marvelous! I'm so happy for Gus. I don't suppose there will be a job for an amateur director with one measly play under her belt in all this?" she asked, worrying about her future.

"Not if I can prevent it!" he said, and laughed. "I don't want you too independent, Ms. Brennan. Of course we'll work something out," he added more seriously. "Have you had breakfast yet?"

"Hours ago."

"Good. Then you're ready to eat again. I just got up. The weather looks decent for a change."

"Yes," she said, but her mind was slipping in another direction, wondering whether he had seen Jessie home. It would be like her to hang around after the others had gone, waiting. Maybe even waiting in Simon's room . . . Never mind, she wasn't going to worry about that. Polite and friendly, period.

"I called you last night," he said.

"Did you? I heard the phone ring but was too tired to get up and answer it."

"Too bad. I was really looking forward to seeing you . . . alone."

He could have been alone with her all today, but this thought too was held back. "What time are we meeting Jessie and Charles?" she asked.

"Around two. Why don't I pick you up and we'll have a bite somewhere before we go."

"Fine."

"Where do you suggest?" he asked. She felt he was hinting to come to her apartment, but that held too much chance for mischief.

"I'll meet you at the hotel. It's such a nice day I feel like a walk."

"I'll pick you up, no trouble."

"I'd rather walk. I'll be there in half an hour."

"All right. I'll order some brunch for us. Can you handle it?"

"That sounds lovely. See you."

She hung up the phone and began her preparations. The black bikini and towel were put into a waterproof tote bag. She selected a flowered sun dress with a removable skirt. That would do for brunch, and later the shorts beneath would be all right for the boat. She scooped her hair up into a chignon against the sea breezes, took up a beach hat and left, willing herself to smile and look forward to the day with some hope of pleasure. It was just a date; she'd enjoy it. Simon was amusing. She didn't get many chances to go out in a motorboat. They'd have dinner at some nice spot afterward. It would be fine if only she could hang on to her heart and her temper—which would start to rise the moment she reflected on Simon's lies about going to his room to make phone calls last night.

He had alerted the waiter she was coming. She was ushered with great pomp to his table, where he sat sipping coffee, jotting notes on a pad.

He arose, took her hand and kissed her fingers in front of the other diners, who smiled their appreciation of his gallantry.

"You were worth waiting for," he said, drawing out her chair. "I told you to wear something sexy, but this is too much. Am I really expected to keep my seat when you come at me looking like this?"

"Down, boy," she ordered. "Is it too low?" she asked, pulling at the top of her sun dress.

"Too low for what? Not too low to suit me, or for style or beauty. A touch risqué for church, I should think. They wouldn't let you anywhere near the Vatican in it, and definitely too low-cut for a man's peace of mind. I love it."

"Since we are going boating, I thought . . ."

"I hope that bag holds the black bikini. I have been looking forward to it all week."

"Yes, I brought it along in case we swim."

"Good. Charles has a bathing pool in his yard. Jessie told me last night."

She stiffened at the intrusion of Jessie's name into the conversation, but forced herself to silence. The waiter came and poured coffee. Soon the food arrived: eggs Benedict, steaming hot under silver food warmers.

"One time-tested way of rating a hotel's cuisine is by its sauces," Simon told her before tasting his food. After the first bite he added, "I would have to give The George a plentiful sprinkling of stars. This is a first-rate hollandaise sauce they serve here."

"Do you eat this well all the time?" she asked.

"Only when I'm working in a civilized country. I have eaten raw fish in Japan; sampled couscous in Arabia; tried beans in Boston, and very smelly cheese and coarse bread in Greece, washed down with a tincture of turpentine called ouzo. When in Rome, you know."

They talked about the party, and the production of Gus's new play. "He'll go into rehearsals with the new cast right after you close here in August. If it takes on TV, he might get it on the stage in the West End. It's more usual to do the live version first, but TV will generate interest in it."

When they had finished, he looked at his watch. "It's only one fifteen. We don't have to be at Wespark till two. Shall we go upstairs for a while?" he asked calmly.

"Have you some phone calls to make?" she asked with an innocent stare.

"No, I have something else in mind," he answered, looking deep into her eyes.

"Let's go for a walk along the beach instead. We don't get many days this nice."

"I have a lovely room—a fine view of the beach."

"I'm so full after brunch, I need the exercise," she insisted.

"You're a hard taskmaster," he said resignedly.

He put on sunglasses and held her hand as they walked along the shingle beach, looking out at the sailboats, the soaring, swooping, noisy gulls; at the youngsters tossing beach balls to and fro. There was an occasional long glance by Simon at the pretty young females working on their tans. Appreciative looks were returned, but with his sunglasses concealing his face, he wasn't recognized.

"I want to have a cottage by the sea one day," Simon said. "Not here, or close to any tourist trap. It should be a nice, private place. Cornwall, maybe."

"You wouldn't find many bikini-clad distractions there," she said, teasing him.

"I only want one distraction," he said, squeezing her fingers.

"You'd miss the attention."

"As a dog misses fleas. I've had more than enough of pretty young things all wanting me to get them a job. It hasn't slipped my attention that you never dunned me for anything."

She adopted a playful air. "Why, I'm only being nice to you so you would give attention to Gus's plays."

"Even when you pretend you're self-seeking, you don't know how to set about it. Gus's plays won't do you much good."

"I might reap some incidental benefit."

"Don't disillusion me. I want to think that *you* are different. And by the way, you haven't been very nice to me lately. Better pull up your socks, or I'll find another girl."

"I wonder who you have in mind."

He pulled her closer to his side, squeezing her hand so hard it hurt. "You are impertinent, Ms. Brennan."

"And *you* are being more macho than is necessary, Mr. Cranston. I have some plans for that set of fingers you're breaking."

"Sorry. I guess I don't know my own strength."

"I don't think you know your own weakness either."

"Meaning?"

"You enjoy being a celebrity—being the famous Simon Cranston pestered by pretty girls, throwing them a few crumbs from your banquet. You'd miss the fleas if you left your job."

"One really bad-natured queen bee could replace all the fleas. We'd better go. We don't want to keep the honorable member waiting."

"Good gracious, no. He might take a pet, and not tell you all the secrets of the Privy Council."

They went back to the hotel, had the car brought out, and were soon driving down the road to Wespark. A pair of wrought-iron gates stood open; a gate house that had once boasted a servant now stood empty. A curved road led to the house, a large stone rectangle that soared three stories into the blue sky. Three rows of mullioned windows blinked in the sun. There were signs of neglect in the grounds, as the parkland was overgrown with bushes and wild grass. Charles and Jessie came out to greet them. Charles accepted their praise of his house, then pointed out some stonework on the third story under the eaves, that was perishing from neglect.

"No one can afford to keep up these large old heaps nowadays. The taxes kill us," he mourned.

A double oak door opened to show them a black-and-white marble floor stretching for several yards before them. There was a curving staircase, and a wall punctuated with ancestors framed in gilt. It was typical of the stately homes of England, with period furnishings and some fine vases in niches along the walls.

"This is the main salon," Charles said, showing them into a room uncomfortably large for four people. Tillie felt lost in it. Its proportions were generous, the room lovely, but signs of its age had begun to show. The fine Aubusson carpet underfoot was threadbare, the velvet draperies at the tall windows fading from the sun.

"Overlooking the state it is in, you can see it was once a fine chamber," he said rather sadly. Running his fingers over a Sheraton table, he showed them a smudge of dust. "In my grandfather's day, we had seventeen house servants and six gardeners. The few servants I can afford aren't able to keep it clean. Of course, they are all bone idle. They don't stir a finger unless I'm here to hound them."

"*I* think it's lovely," Jessie said. "Charles doesn't live in this part of the house. He has a modern apartment he spends all his time in. Why don't you get us a drink, Charles?"

"If we plan to go out in the boat, we should do it now. The wind is rising," Tillie mentioned.

"Can I take the wheel?" Jessie asked.

"'*May* I take the wheel' is what you should have said," Charles reproved gently. "If you hope to inhabit decent society, my dear, you must express yourself properly."

"Isn't he awful?" Jessie laughed. "But I asked him to correct me. I was never any good at grammar."

"We'll go down to the sea now if you like," Charles said.

They walked through the park, down to a wharf with a boat house. The launch was made of mahogany, a large craft, new and expensive. Tillie thought that if her house was falling apart, she would spend her extra money on refurbishing it before she would buy a thing like this.

"It must be a gas-guzzler," Simon said unthinkingly.

"It is. I don't drive it much. It's a toy, really," Charles admitted. "Isn't that how some wag defined the difference between men and boys? The price of their toys."

The waves increased as the wind blew stronger. The boat slapped against the guards, which protected it from being smashed against the boat house.

"I really think we ought to wait for a calmer day," Charles told them, glancing out to sea.

"Why don't we do that?" Simon agreed at once. "I, for one, would love to have a look around your house. I have some interest in these old historical homes."

Tillie was disappointed; Jessie pouted and complained. They had come for a motorboat ride, and at the first sign of a wave, it was canceled. They went back to the house and entered by a different door which led into Charles's private living quarters. The antique furnishings and décor gave way to modern, functional appointments. There was a wall of hi-fi equipment, and facing it a grouping of low, mushroom-colored sofas. Modern abstract paintings were on the walls, a Scandinavian rug plush underfoot.

"I recognize the hand of Paromi in this room," Simon said. "I did a show on him once. His interiors are charming. In fact, he did my London living room for me. You've seen it, Jessie."

"You both use the same decorator?" she asked, always interested to know the names of the famous and near-famous.

"I believe our tastes are rather similar," Charles

said, smiling. "But it is the older part of the house you are interested in, Simon. Let's have a quick tour."

They went through library and sitting rooms, studies, bedchambers, withdrawing rooms. "Two monarchs and three princes have laid their heads on that goose-feather pillow," Charles said proudly. "It nearly bankrupted my great-great-grandfather entertaining one of the Georges—George the Fourth, I think it was."

"Entertaining him would be enough to do it," Simon said, nodding. "He's the fellow who had the Royal Pavilion at Brighton built."

A desk was pointed out as having belonged to Marie Antoinette; a pair of crossed swords over a fireplace were a gift to an ancestor from the Duke of Wellington; an epergne on a table was from one of the Princes of Wales. With such a lot of valuable pieces that could be sold at auction, Tillie wondered that Charles so often lamented his lack of money. She must remember to tell Gus he was mistaken in thinking Charles had been involved in any bribery. He wouldn't complain about his financial embarrassment so much if he had.

They went next to the art gallery, a long room with delicate pillars at regular intervals, giving it the air of a portico.

"This marble bust that guards the doorway was won in a card game by my gambling ancestor. From that same royal gentleman who built the Pavilion," Charles said, running his hand over its cool smoothness. "It is by Canova—a beautiful thing, in its way. Fairly invites you to feel and touch and imagine what female posed for it."

"She had a big nose, whoever she was," Jessie pointed out.

"The child has no aesthetic values. None," Charles apologized.

"Sure I have, Charles. They're just different from yours," Jessie answered saucily.

"Mine are informed, but then it is not *your* fault that your family didn't educate you in these matters. You are bright—I shall teach you."

"That looks like a Vandyke," Simon said, pointing across the room. They all strolled toward the painting.

"Yes, one of my ancestors was painted by Vandyke when he was working in England. The family resemblance still lingers, I'm told. I wore an outfit like the one in this painting to the Duchess of Tavistock's costume party last year, thinking I had an original notion. But several ladies and gentlemen had also dressed like their ancestors. Great minds think alike."

"If that's a genuine Rembrandt hanging beside your ancestor, your money troubles are over," Simon said, strolling to the next exhibit to examine a rather ugly woman whose face emerged from a gloomy brown background. The details were hard to distinguish, the gown melding into the walls behind her.

"No such luck. It's the school of Rembrandt, but not by the master," Charles told him. "I've several near-famous artists, but it would be a desecration to break up the collection. It belongs in the family. If I had any money, I'd add to it. The early nineteenth-century artists are going at good prices. They'll certainly appreciate sharply, or so my dealer tells me."

"Sotheby?" Simon asked.

"Good gracious, no. I can't afford the very best. You get a better bargain foraging around the smaller shops—and perferably not in London. The Continent still has some treasures hidden here and there. Not that I have either the time or money to do much. It's a sort of hobby. There is always the hope, too, that you'll find a real masterpiece hiding under several centuries of dust and grime."

"It happens occasionally," Simon agreed, nodding. "There was a fellow in Italy who bought a Tintoretto for an old song last year. You'd have to know a lot about art to spot a thing like that."

"I don't believe I flatter myself unduly in saying I know a little something about art at least," Charles said. "When you grow up surrounded by these things, you pick up an appreciation—if you aren't born with it. Some natures are just too vulgar to be taught. There are, unfortunately, those among us who will always hang tigers painted on black velvet in their rooms and fancy themselves art lovers."

"I never was much interested in art, myself. If I had any money to spare, I'd collect old classic cars," Simon said.

"They've already gone through the roof," Charles told him. "The money has been made on old cars. The restoration is very expensive too. No, you can't make money on cars, but painting is still a possibility."

"Have you had any luck in this endeavor so far?"

"The bathing pool in the backyard is from one of my coups. I found a small Chardin in a shop in Brussels. Paid roughly two hundred pounds for it, and sold it for ten times that sum. I hated to part with it, but at the time I was young and foolish and thought a pool a necessary part of a bachelor's equipment. Last year I sold a few bits of bric-a-brac and bought the boat."

"That must have been very elegant bric-a-brac," Jessie ventured.

"Some Meissen porcelain that I particularly disliked. A Sèvres vase, a few things like that. The boat was going very cheap. A chap was about to declare bankruptcy and wanted to sell off what chattels he could and hide the money, to keep it from the creditors."

"Very wise," Simon said, but to Tillie it sounded more criminal than wise.

"I am not quite on the verge of bankruptcy," Charles assured them, "but I daresay Wespark will end up in the hands of the National Trust one day. Seems a shame an estate that has been in the family for hundreds of years must be lost, but I won't be the first to suffer."

"Why don't you rent the gate house?" Tillie asked. "It's not occupied, is it? I noticed there were no curtains at the front of the place."

"It is uninhabitable. I'd have to spend a fortune on roofing and repairs. It would take years to recoup the investment. But enough of my sad financial condition. What shall we drink? Sherry? A brandy for you, Simon?"

"Let's have champagne," Jessie suggested.

"That is for very special occasions, dear girl. I have only half a dozen bottles left in the wine cellar."

Tillie found the ways of the wealthy who thought they were poor very strange. Brandy and champagne, new motor launches and fancy cars, and a house in decay.

"We really should get out to the pool while the sun is up," Jessie said, glancing out the window. "The wind won't bother us. We can swim and sunbathe. My tan is fading."

"This penchant the young women have for tanning their hides baffles me. A maidenly pallor is far more becoming," Charles told her.

"You're old-fashioned."

"If you say so, my dear. In that case, it isn't sherry or brandy we shall want, but a tall, cool drink. How about a nice Pimm's for the ladies?" Charles offered graciously.

"How about the same for the gentlemen? Or this one, at least," Simon added.

"Good. We'll change and have a servant bring them to us," he decreed. "There's a pair of cabanas by the pool to change in, if you like. My bathing gear is there."

They went through a hallway, out a door to a private garden, walled around on two sides by open-worked stone, with greenery giving privacy on the other side. An oval pool glittered like a jewel in the sun. Padded iron chairs sat in a cluster around a table at the pool's edge. Charles showed the women to one cabana; he and Simon went to the other.

"I wouldn't mind living in this changing house," Jessie said, looking around the spacious room with one mirrored wall. There were wicker chairs and a sofa with brightly padded cushions.

"Maybe he'll rent it to you," Tillie answered jokingly.

"He doesn't like renting any part of the ancestral acres. He kicked the couple out of the gate house last year, he told me. They were destroying the place. She painted two bedrooms bile green. Good oak paneling, imagine, and she painted two rooms green without asking him."

"That's a lot of gall."

"He only let them have the place because he needed the money. He says he'd rather be poor than put up with that."

"He's rather snobbish, isn't he?"

"Yes, and his sister is worse. They think because they know their grandparents' history it makes them special. Silly asses."

They changed into their bathing suits. Jessie wore a

one-piece white suit, cut as low as possible above, and as high below. Tillie wore her black bikini, which looked so brief that she took a white terry-cloth robe from the wall and put it on top before going out.

"I'm not going to swim," Jessie said, lifting back her hair. "I don't want to get my hair wet, and I refuse to wear a bathing cap in front of the men. Are you swimming?"

"We got gypped out of our ride in the motorboat; I'm going to swim."

"You didn't bring a cap."

"Maybe Charles has a hair dryer. He has everything else."

The servant had just arrived with their drinks when they went out. The men were waiting for them at the table under an umbrella.

"I want some sun," Jessie said. "I'm going to lie down on that divine lounge bed with my drink at my elbow and just soak up the heat like a lizard."

"An extremely unlikely comparison, my dear," Charles said, his eyes admiring her smooth lines. "I shall take the other lounge beside you. I see Tillie isn't planning to sunbathe," he added, looking at her terry-cloth robe.

"I borrowed this from your cabana. I hope you don't mind."

"*I* don't, but I have a suspicion Simon minds very much," he said with a playful leer at Simon. "Your maidenly modesty is very becoming. Not many young women nowadays possess that . . . *refinement.*" After this compliment, he lounged off to the unrefined Jessica, with every appearance of pleasure.

"What a phony," Tillie said in a low voice.

"I agree, but he's right about my not liking the terry-cloth robe. I'm eager for a view of the black bikini."

"You should have told me. I would have shown it to you before I put it on."

He pulled a chair back for her. While at her side, he calmly removed the beach coat and threw it on a chair. "Nothing to hide there," he said, lifting his brows in approval. "Shall I put down the umbrella and let the sun bake us?"

"All right."

"These things are purposely designed by vicious engineers to break your fingers," he complained, struggling with the mechanism. "There, that's got it."

They arranged their chairs to face the fullest of the sun's rays and sipped their drinks, looking around at the garden surrounding the pool.

"Charles is going broke in style," he commented idly.

"Isn't he though? You'd think he'd fix up the family home, since it means so much to him. I would, if it were mine. Though it *is* lovely to have a private pool," she sighed happily.

"Do you really think we'd do much swimming on the wind-swept coast of Cornwall?"

"Cornwall? Who said anything about Cornwall?"

"Haven't we more or less settled on a cozy cottage in the country, with me typing away on my *chef-d'oeuvre* while you fry eggs and bake bread and raise the kids?"

"No, Simon, we haven't. *I* plan to be a great director, remember? Ms. Brennan is the name."

"Ms. Cranston has a good ring to it, too."

She peered at him, wondering why he should hint at marriage when he was plainly interested in women other than her. Or maybe the word Ms. implied no more than a housemate, unmarried. In any case, they were not well enough acquainted to speak of marriage.

He lifted his sunglasses and smiled. "Did I scare you?"

"Oh no, I'm not that timid. In fact, I'm feeling brave enough to tackle the pool. How about you?"

"Any fear of that bikini shrinking? I'll stand by with towels if it does. I don't want anyone but me seeing that much of you."

"It's been wet before. It doesn't shrink," she said, setting down her drink.

They went to the edge of the pool, tested the water with their toes. "Are you two coming in?" Tillie called to the others.

"Maybe later. Jessie and I are considering getting deliciously drunk. It's so easy in the sunlight. I don't know why, but the liquor goes straight to your head. Drink up, Jess," Charles said.

Tillie began sliding in, inch by inch, not wanting to wet her hair.

"A coward dies many deaths," Simon told her. "The only way is to dive in and suffer the heart attack all at once."

"You talk a good game."

"Are you challenging my courage, woman? Never let it be said a Cranston refused a challenge. Have warm blankets and brandy at the ready. This pool is not heated." He braced himself and dove in, disappearing from sight for what seemed a long time, only to emerge at the other end, howling with shock at the cold temperature.

"Charles, you dog, what a way to treat guests!" he called. "This water is like ice."

"Sorry, old chap. The heater is broken," he called back. "You get used to it after a while."

"The numbness is setting in now. I think my feet are frozen solid."

"Maybe I won't go in after all," Tillie decided, withdrawing the one foot she had immersed.

Simon suddenly began swimming back to her end of the pool, his head in the water, arms flashing. Within seconds, he was at the pool's edge, climbing out to grasp Tillie's arms in his wet, cold hands.

"Whose idea was it we go in for a swim?" he asked, lowering his head to drip very cold water on her. "Yours! *I* was content to sip my drink in the sun like a civilized human being. *You* shamed me into it, and don't think you're going to escape unfrozen, young lady."

"Simon, don't!" she shrieked, pulling away. "You're freezing me."

They wrestled a moment, precariously, at the edge of the pool. He let go of her arms, only to encircle her body. They felt like icy tentacles. She writhed and squirmed, but in the end the inevitable happened. They went splashing together into the cold water, to come up coughing and spluttering.

"You did that on purpose!" she babbled. "Oh, my hair is ruined. Simon, I'll kill you."

"First you'll have to catch me," he said, and darted away to the other end of the pool, his dark head streaking along in the water.

She swam after him, knowing it was impossible to keep pace. They became accustomed to the coldness after a few moments. It was refreshing, invigorating, with the warm sun above and the cool water below. They played in the water like children, chasing, ducking, and swimming underwater. Tillie's hair became unbound.

"You look like a mermaid when you swim underwater with your hair streaming out behind. Care to entice me beneath and ravish me?"

When they had had enough and got out, they saw

Charles and Jessie arising to leave the pool area. "We're going to make arrangements for dinner," Charles called.

"Where do you girls want to go?" Simon asked. "Maybe we should make reservations."

"We're eating here," Jessie called back.

"I hope *she's* not cooking," Simon said when they had left.

"I assume you've tried her cooking?" Tillie asked, feeling a dash of jealousy. It was hard to go on trying not to love Simon, when he was acting like himself.

"Only her coffee. I mean real coffee—the kind that comes in cups."

"Ah yes, that beverage you usually take for breakfast."

"On that occasion, I took it at night. Jess puts oil in her coffee. Or possibly soda. It was both bubbly and oily."

"She doesn't have a percolator. She boils the coffee right in the pan with the water."

"That explains the mystery of the foreign bodies I found at the botom of my cup. I thought perhaps she got some sand in her oil. Let my dry you," he offered, taking a large beach towel to rub her back and arms.

"Not so hard," she complained.

"I *do* seem to rub you the wrong way, no matter what I do. Why don't I stop rubbing?" he asked, tossing the towel aside to take her in his arms.

His body was still cold and wet, making her minutely aware of its pressure against her. His hands on her bare skin moved along the curve of her waist, then went around her to pull her more tightly against him. Her plans of a politely friendly afternoon blew away at his touch. The intimacy of their near-naked bodies locked together fired her with desire. She thought of the private beach they had never got to, and knew that if they were alone at this moment, she would gladly surrender herself to him. She was grateful for the saving knowledge of Charles's and Jessie's presence nearby, possibly observing them right now from some window.

"Simon, don't," she said, disengaging herself reluctantly. "It's too public here."

He looked around at the walls, the banks of yews and hollies. "I've heard walls have ears, but surely not eyes," he pointed out. "If you don't want to be touched, you shouldn't look so tempting. How is a fellow supposed to keep his hands off you, with all those supple curves inviting a caress?" It was only his gaze that touched her, but it was an intimate, disconcerting look.

"A regular marble statue in that respect," she said breathlessly.

"Not so cold and lifeless," he objected, placing a kiss below her ear, where it set off a chain reaction deep within. Her arms went around him as if by their own volition. At this response, he swept her tightly to him and she thrilled to the firm pressure of his chest, rough with hair, against hers. One of his hands traveled the lineaments of those curves he had been admiring, gliding slowly, in a leisurely way, down her rib cage to the indentation of her waist, the swell of hips. His fingers tightened a moment, then went around her to massage the small of her back, while she molded herself to him. Her hips, her thighs, were brushing his, and she moved, uncontrollably against him.

He didn't kiss her, but gazed into her eyes while she looked back at him. Then his eyes lowered to her lips and lingered there a disturbing moment, while she waited for his kiss. "So sweet," he murmured softly. As if in slow motion, his head inclined till their lips brushed, no more. Her nerves stretched taut, her body tingled in an exquisite agony of anticipation.

"Simon!" she said impatiently, and moved to kiss him soundly. His subsequent attack repaid her waiting. She was caught in a rib-crushing bear hug that squeezed the very breath from her. She felt the beat of his heart against her own, a wild, tumultuous beat that reverberated in her ears, while her lips were bruised by the pressure of his.

For a long time they kissed, heedless of windows and watchers, oblivious to everything but the perturbing swell of emotion that held them.

When his fingers reached for the strings of her bikini top to undo them, she returned, reluctantly, to her senses.

"Simon, what would anyone think if they saw us!"

"I doubt they're wasting any time looking at us. How long do you think it takes to tell the cook to toss a couple of steaks on the grill? Those two are doing just what we should be doing."

"Now be a good boy. Sit down and drink your drink, before it gets warm," she ordered, leading him to a chair, where he promptly pulled her onto his lap. She jumped up and went to her own chair, taking her drink with her to prevent his further molesting her.

His eyes were dark, smoldering with desire, but his lips were smiling. "What do you think of Charles?" he asked.

"I've already told you. Phony."

"I think he's a liar. Good taste, though. I don't suppose it's the thing to do: accept a man's hospitality, then rip him up behind his back. Would you like to go for a stroll?"

"In this?" she asked, looking down at her bikini.

"Oh no, we don't want to scandalize the scenery. Put on your robe."

She reached for it, then realized the imperative nature of his speech and dropped it. "I'm going to stay here and take some sun," she said.

"Please? That was a suggestion, not an order. I know you modern Ms.'s don't take to commands with any facility at all. Come on, don't be stubborn," he said, arising and taking the robe to place over her shoulders.

"Where do you want to go?" she asked.

"Let's stroll down toward the road, through the park."

She sensed he wanted to get away to a more private spot. He would kiss her, but he could hardly do more, and as her own inclination ran in the same path, she didn't object. He took her hand, and they walked off. It was soon evident his mind was not on romance. He set off at a brisk pace, straight down to the gate house.

"It's pretty," she said, looking at the stone building. It had leaded windows, and large concrete quoins.

"Charming," he agreed, walking all around.

"You seem more than a little interested in it."

"I am very much interested in it. I don't see anything wrong with the roof, either."

"You can't see the roof from here."

"I can see the edges. And from the top of the hill on the way down I saw undamaged slate shingles. That roof looks okay to me, better than the one on the main building."

"He'd rent it if it was in good shape. He could use the money, to hear him talk. Anyway, it's none of our business. Let's go back."

"I was hoping he'd rent it to me. You know what a keen interest I'm taking in Brighton this summer. I wouldn't mind having a *pied-à-terre* near here."

"Why don't you ask him? You would have to

promise not to paint anything green. He ejected the last tenant for that stunt."

"Where did you hear that?" he asked with a sharp look at her.

"Jessie told me."

"When did it happen?"

"Last year. Why?"

"Nothing. Don't mention to him I spoke of renting it."

"You're acting funny, Simon."

"It was just an idea. I guess it doesn't make much sense. It would be cheaper to stay in the hotel on weekends. I wouldn't be able to come down often during the week, with my nightly show to prepare. Besides, I *like* green," he added jocularly. "I wouldn't want to have digs I couldn't paint green."

They strolled back up the hill toward the house and pool, stopping to look at birds and squirrels, with Simon selecting which specimens he would allow near his cottage in Cornwall.

"You sound as if you really plan to move to Cornwall one day," she said.

"I do. Don't you like Cornwall?"

"I've never seen it."

"You'll like it," he said, tightening his hold on her hand very calmly, as though it were all settled they would be going there to live together. But he hadn't really asked her to marry him.

"Don't say anything to Charles about where we've been," he said as they approached the pool. "It would look as though we were snooping."

It was not possible to say anything. Neither Charles nor Jessie was there, but they soon came out, carrying fresh drinks for everyone.

"We're having steaks and salad," Jessie announced. "Charles and I chose them personally. Well marbled and delicious, and very bad for the heart, Charles tells me."

"With a surprise for dessert," Charles added.

They conversed easily while they had their drinks, then they changed back into their regular clothing for dinner.

Chapter Seven

Over dinner they spoke, appropriately, of food. It was international cuisine being discussed, which left the two women the role of listeners.

"I didn't realize you had traveled so much, Charles," Jessie commented.

"I haven't been around the world, by any means. We MP's get a few perks, you know. Commonwealth missions, trade and defense meetings. I've been around a bit."

But his anecdotes did not sound like work trips. It was difficult to imagine how a luau in Hawaii, for instance, had anything to do with his job. Intermingled with the talk of food, he spoke of skiing, night-clubbing and going to shows in New York. Charles, Tillie decided, was not a very serious member of parliament.

"We really must take these charming women to

Paris, Simon," he said later on. "It is so much more comfortable traveling with ladies."

Instead of having to pick up some ladies after you get there, Tillie finished mentally, for that was what he meant.

He was fussy about his wine, and proud of it. He showed the label to Simon, pointing out the vintage and the vineyard from which it had come. "I never serve anything but a good French wine with steak," he said. "You may get away with Italian or Portuguese or Spanish with a highly-spiced dish, but steak betrays its weakness."

The meal was delicious, if uninspired in choice. They had a salad and crusty rolls. "If my cook were here, we would have something more civilized," Charles apologized, "but these fellows expect their two days a week off now, as though they were gentlemen, and not common laborers. In my grandfather's day, they got half a day a week if they were fortunate. We're ready for dessert now," he said aside to the servant who waited on his table, in hearing of Charles's remarks about the working class.

Dessert was a raspberry fool, delicious, and grossly fattening. It was a concoction of fresh fruit and whipped cream, liberally laced with various liqueurs and served in fluted crystal sherbet glasses. All his porcelain and silver were of the finest.

"I was taught to appreciate the finer things of life," he admitted when complimented on the meal. "Good food and wine, fine paintings, beautiful women," he added, patting Jessie's hand. She took no exception to being put into a class with these inanimate objects, but Tillie felt an urge to squelch him.

"I have a delightful liqueur I picked up in Paris. Shall we go into the drawing room and sample it?" he invited, very much the gracious host.

"My head is spinning already," Jessie objected.

"A *lady* must learn how to hold her liquor," he told her.

She struggled gamely to her feet, and they all went into the other room.

He lifted a decanter holding a green-colored liquid. "Absinthe," he announced grandly. "It's potent stuff. In fact, it's credited with the destruction of a few famous artists in Paris, where I got it."

"I thought it was forbidden in France," Simon mentioned.

"I believe you are right. It must be Amsterdam where I picked it up. Strange city. With all those islands and canals, it has no feeling at all of Venice."

"You should have picked me up a diamond while you were there," Jessie said, joking. "Isn't that where people get diamonds?"

"It used to be the best place to get them cut, before the war," Charles said. "After the occupation, many of the craftsmen went to New York or London. Marvelous stuff, this absinthe, but sip gently, ladies. It can cause debility."

"I'll pass, thanks," Tillie said.

"Simon, you are not afraid of the wicked drink?" he challenged.

"I'll give it a try," Simon said, passing his glass.

"We'll have some Irish Cream, eh Tillie?" Jessie offered, making herself at home at the liquor cabinet.

"A very small one, thanks."

"What's in this?" Simon asked, tasting carefully, with no noticeable pleasure.

"The leaf and flower tops of wormwood, angelica root, anise, other things," Charles said, sipping with great contentment. "One feels very much the roué, so dissipated, imbibing a forbidden drink," he rambled on. "Have you ever noticed, Simon, how the government bans all the good things? You ought to do a show on it. As sure as a truly delightful play is introduced, some bunch of housewives get together and proclaim it indecent. They've banned topless bathing at many beaches in the world now. All drugs are taboo. A man can't indulge his civilized tastes for the crushing taxes imposed on us all—all of us who had anything to start off with. I'd like to know what *you* pay the government in pennies and pounds per annum."

"I'd like to *have* what I pay," Simon agreed, laughing, but not volunteering the information.

"Yes, by Jove, they want to equalize us all. Raise up the lowest sod-crusher to the level of a gentleman. You can't make a silk purse of a sow's ear, and vice versa. They want to grind us into the mud, demmed taxes."

"It's your government that's doing it," Tillie pointed out.

"*My* government? Not the Tories. It was the Labor Party that destroyed the country."

"You're in power now. Why don't you do something about it?" she asked.

"I should, by Jove, I should," he said, pouring another dollop of absinthe into his glass. "Simon? Have another, do. Keep me company," he urged.

Tillie was unhappy to see Simon quaff his drink and pass his glass for a refill. Charles was becoming quite tipsy. His speech was beginning to slur.

"Hard for a man to save a penny, with the heavy taxes," Simon said in a supporting way.

"Hard? It's impossible. An honest man can't do it."

"Even a dishonest one would have to be clever," Simon said.

"He would, by Jove," he agreed, taking another drink. "Swiss bank account—They can't touch that. I fancy *you* have a Swiss account, Simon? A fellow in your position, making a fortune for just smiling and talking on the telly."

"I do a little more than that."

In the befuddled state he was in, Charles failed to notice he hadn't really gotten an answer to his question. "Swiss account," he said, nodding. "Next thing you do, you move to Ireland and set yourself up as a creative artist. They have no income tax on creative artists in Ireland, you know. A man could have a civilized existence, I daresay."

"But then you would have to create something," Jessie pointed out. "Writers, artists, that sort of thing. You can't write, can you?"

"No, but I can smear paint on the canvas as well as the next one. No law says you have to sell what you create. Be a non-selling artist," he said, taking another sip and smacking his lips.

"You wouldn't want to leave Wespark," Tillie pointed out. "Your ancestral home for hundreds of years."

"Can't afford it. It eats up every penny I make. Will fall into the National Trust soon, the rate I'm going. Foolish to put another penny into it. Let it go to rack and ruin. I'll pick it clean of its treasures and let 'em have it. Ideal solution. 'Pon my word it is," he said, his eyelids sagging.

"But first, one has to accumulate this wealth to deposit in Switzerland," Simon pointed out. "It's difficult, because of the taxes."

"More than one way to skin a cat. Have another drink, Simon old boy. Hold your liquor like a gentleman, even if you're—" He wisely stopped then.

"Not?" Simon finished for him, making it a question.

"I think we'd better be going, Simon," Tillie said, fearing a fight would soon break out.

"Very soon. Charles and I are just going to have one for the road, eh Charles? Not every night I get to drink absinthe."

"Charles does every night, nearly," Jessie said, smiling. "Will you take me home, Simon? I'm afraid to let him drive me."

"Certainly," Simon said, not only happily, but eagerly. Tillie felt the old jealousy set in again, and a revulsion at what Simon was doing, getting Charles drunk to discover news from him.

"I'm not much good at skinning cats myself," Simon said, leaning back in his chair in a leisurely way. "If you have any secrets, Charles, I wish you'd pass them along. How do you figure I could put a few pounds away without the government's getting wind of it?"

"Don't know much about your business. You travel about. Must be some way you could bank your money in another country. Set yourself up as a corporation. Simon Cranston, Incorporated."

"I've already done that."

"Don't hide your money in a sugar bowl. It won't be worth anything in ten years, with the inflation. Buy something—anything. Gold, jewelry, antiques—but not real estate. The taxes are crippling. Something you can haul off to Ireland with you. We'll set up as painters, eh Simon? Paint the ladies," he said smiling, in a stupor.

"Simon, let's go," Tillie repeated.

"Go? Rubbish. The night's young," Charles said, but his eyelids were sliding closed.

"So am I, and I'd like to live till I'm a little older. I think it's time to go," Jessie said.

"My pillow, dear, before you go. My favorite pillow," Charles said, slumping down on the sofa.

Jessie selected a plump velvet cushion and slid it

under his head. "It's his comforter, like a teddy bear or blanket," she explained. "He even takes it to bed with him."

She called the butler, who was not greatly surprised to see the honorable member snoozing on the sofa with the glass of absinthe tilting dangerously in his fingers. He removed it, and saw the party to the door.

"Does he do this often?" Tillie asked.

"Fairly often. That's why I always suggest champagne. He doesn't pass out on it, but only gets happy."

"Why do you bother with him?" Tillie asked.

"He knows people. The right people. And he's fairly harmless, you know. I mean, a fellow who passes out every night isn't very demanding."

"How do you get home after visiting him?"

"I call a taxi from the city, and get money from Charles to pay for it. But we don't come here often. Sometimes I get him to drop me off before he comes home. Speaking of dropping off, you know where my flat is, Simon. You can leave me there. Would you two like to come up for some coffee?"

"I still have to make a trip to London tonight. I think we'd better pass," Simon answered.

After she'd gotten out, he said to Tillie, "Of course, if *you* want to ask me in, that's a different matter entirely."

"You really should have something before driving back. I don't know about you, but my head's spinning from all the drinks. Pimm's all afternoon, wine with dinner, and then liqueur. To say nothing of the stuff in that dessert. Wasn't it good?"

"The absinthe was like paint remover."

"You took two glasses. Why were you goading Charles on to get drunk?"

"Why, you never know what an honorable mem-

ber will come out with when he's under the influence.
You haven't forgotten why we endured his dull company for the whole day, have you?"

"No, but you didn't do a very good job of picking his brains. You didn't find out much."

"Wrong, dummy. I found out what I want to know . . . nearly."

"What was that?"

"Tune in to the Simon Cranston show."

"Tomorrow night?"

"No, give me a week or so to check it out. I only broadcast facts, ma'am, not innuendo. It's what separates the gossip mongers from the big boys, and it also saves a lot on libel and slander suits."

"You're going to do an exposé on how expensive and incompetent our members of parliament are, aren't you? I think it's shocking if he uses our tax money to go to Hawaii just to party."

"What *I* am wondering is what possible excuse he found to go to Amsterdam."

"And Paris, and New York, and all those other places. Some gentleman—He makes such a point of being one."

"He has to. All he has left is the name, and the tarnished glory of his family. Sad, really, but then he doesn't need pity. He started off with it all. If he's slipped into this state, it's his fault. I'd rather be what I am. I didn't object to his hint I wasn't a gentleman, knowing what the word meant to him: himself."

"And what are you?"

"Just a man. A farmer's son. I inherited my father's ugly looks, and my Irish mother's silver tongue that makes me a living. I guess I also got lucky. To be fair, I shall add I have worked like a demon since I was old enough to know I wanted more out of life than herding cattle, like my dad."

He pulled the Bentley into the curb in front of her apartment house. "Am I invited in?" he asked.

"Yes, I need your arm to steady me as I mount the two flights of stairs. My head is reeling."

"I *do* hate to see a pretty young girl fall down dead drunk in the street. Especially when she is *my* girl. No collapsing till I get you inside the front door, understand?"

With her mind muddled by the drinks, she said more than she intended. "Your girl, singular? One of your girls, you mean."

"You're looking at a one-woman man, Tillie. You're probably seeing two of me now, but if you see two girls, take another look. They're both gorgeous brunettes named Ms. Tillie Brennan."

"I bet you say that to all the girls," she said, stifling a yawn.

"Bet again. I'm going to sober you up before I go home."

"No, no, *I* am going to sober *you* up so you don't drive that expensive car into the sea."

"What would you miss, the car or me?"

"You," she answered without having to think.

He walked up the narrow staircase behind her, "to catch you if you keel over," as he bluntly put it.

"Where's the coffee kept?" he asked when they went in.

"In the kitchen. I'll make it."

"I'll make it. You rest," he ordered, leading her to the sofa, where she leaned her head back against the pillows and felt the room wheel around in circles. She heard, as if from a distance, the clatter of cans and pots and cups in the kitchen. The great Simon Cranston, Incorporated is making coffee for me, she thought, with a dazed smile. Soon he appeared beside her.

"In ten minutes, it'll be ready. That gives me ten minutes of your undivided attention," he said, sitting beside her.

"I never had coffee made for me by a corporation before," she told him, smiling a wobbly smile.

"Have you ever been kissed by a corporation?" he asked, drawing her into his arms.

"Never. Not even a company, or partnership."

"Fasten your safety belt," he warned, and kissed her, laying her down on the sofa and stretching out close beside her. His hands moved over her shoulders, sliding down the straps of her sun dress. He kissed her neck, her shoulders, and tugged her dress down far enough to expose the rosy crests of her breasts, which he quickly covered again with his mouth. She felt as though she were on a merry-go-round, a beautiful carousel, with Simon rising above her, on top of her, kissing her, telling her she was beautiful, that he loved her and wanted her.

She splayed her hands wide over his shoulders, savoring his male strength, the hard muscles that knotted into prominence and shifted to valleys as he moved. Sliding her hands over his body, she explored the soft texture of his lips and skin as opposed to the rough line of his jaw.

He grabbed one hand and pressed it to his lips. "I suppose you realize you're driving me crazy," he said, his voice ragged with repressed emotion. "These hands are lethal weapons. They kill me."

"Kiss me, you fool," she cooed.

His hot lips ignited her, till she was moving against him, encouraging him, forgetting her intentions. Good resolutions were irrelevant in the face of the violent emotions that rose to engulf her, as they rode the riptide of desire.

"Simon, Simon," she heard someone say in her

voice—but a different, breathless, longing voice. "I love you so much. I want you."

He disengaged himself and stood up to scoop her into his arms. She tucked her head under his chin and was carried into the bedroom and tossed lightly onto the bed. She slid off her sun dress while he disrobed, then he came to her. The dim light from the window engulfed him in shadows, showing her only a dark profile. When he took her into his arms she gave an involuntary shiver at the intimacy of the feeling of warm skin against skin. She had never made love before, but in her imaginings, she had thought it would be like this: a raging, delirious fever that made her forget for the moment everything but her desire for this man, who cradled her gently, as though she was precious to him.

With one arm still holding her, Simon shifted his position till his head hovered above hers. "Oh, I've been looking forward to this. This is going to be a night to remember," he said softly.

"Is that what Simon says?" she asked with a coquettish laugh.

His arms tightened around her. "Simon says . . ." he began, but never completed the sentence. His lips descended on hers, carrying her along on the swelling tide of passion. She felt strangely afloat on a billowing sea that surged and cascaded and swelled as his hands found out the evocative secret places that aroused her. Unfamiliar ripples of feeling rushed along her nerve endings as he stroked her body, caressed her thighs, then ebbed when he moved his hands to her back, only to inundate her again when he electrified her neck with nuzzling kisses. She strained against him, feeling an urge to drown herself in the maelstrom of his love. She was on the edge of insanity from wanting him.

"Simon, is this real?" she sighed, "or am I tipsy? I always hoped it would be like this when I finally—"

She felt his body stiffen. "What do you mean?"

"Nothing. Kiss me again."

He kissed her, but gently. "Darling, are you telling me this is the first time—"

"Of course. What did you think?"

A low moan escaped his lips. "I can't."

"What's the matter?"

"Everything," he said grimly, "including the fact that you, my lovely love, are not entirely sober."

"I'm sober as a judge!"

"No, *tomorrow* you will be sober and judge me differently than you do tonight."

The stove bell chose that moment to begin its toll.

"Whew. Saved by the bell," he said, withdrawing himself from her arms. "It's not coffee I need, but a cold shower."

"I feel suddenly as if I've already had one of those. Are you leaving, then?" she asked, piqued.

"Leaving your bed temporarily. As our pal General MacArthur said, 'I shall return.' Honey, I can wait and do things right."

"I don't want to wait."

"Not another word of encouragement, woman. I'm not made of forged steel, but fallible, weak human tissue. Get up and make yourself decent. Put on the most concealing robe you own. Sit well away from me. We are going to have coffee; then I am going to get painfully into my car and drive to the hotel. Period."

He did as he said, only drawing her into his arms just before he left for one last kiss. "Let's allow ourselves this last moment of torment," he said. "I don't know whether this is heaven or hell, but I know it's unreal. Now I have it! Purgatory. A place of temporary suffering, but with paradise to look forward to."

He held her face between his two hands for a moment, gazing at her, then he closed his eyes and kissed her on the lips and left.

Chapter Eight

Upon consideration, Tillie decided Simon had behaved like a perfect gentleman. He must really love her, or he would have taken advantage of her tipsy condition and her willingness to have him make love to her. He would be in Brighton often now. If he called on the spur of the moment next time, she wouldn't be such an idiot. She'd agree to see him.

Jessie spoke of the double date on Monday afternoon, when she came for the rehearsal. "Has Simon gone home yet?" she asked.

"Yes, he left last night. Why do you ask?"

"I was just wondering if he stayed at your place overnight."

"No, he didn't," Tillie answered, incensed at the impertinence of the question.

"If he calls again, remind him about Paris. Won't it

be super? If I know Charles and Simon, we'll stay at one of the very posh hotels and go to all the right places for entertainment."

"Don't wait for Simon and me to accompany you, Jessie. Charles will take you alone if that's what you really want."

"Oh, but that's *not* what I want, darling. I would *much* rather go with Simon—and you, of course," she added with an ironic smile.

The rehearsal for her play went better when Tillie used Larry Moss's advice and gave it a farcical twist. Jessie liked it better too, as she was then able to use her voice and body in the exaggerated way that was natural to her. There was no point in being subtle when Jessie was your tool.

Simon phoned Monday night after the performance. "I'm just checking up to see if you're at home and not out with the Muscle."

"If I had known that, I wouldn't have answered my phone," she replied, easy in her mind now and able to be perfectly natural with him.

"Did you catch my show tonight?"

"Yes, I came home after rehearsal and had dinner in my flat, just to see you. You were very good."

"This is grossly unfair, you know. You can see me every night at six if you want, but I won't get to see you. I'm an idiot. I should have taken some pictures Sunday—moving pictures."

"You have me on that first taped interview with Gus, unless you threw it out."

"I have it. I've watched it a couple of times, but it's painful to watch me making such a jackass of myself. Besides, it doesn't look like you, with all the makeup. Pretty, but not *you*."

"Next time we'll take some pictures."

"For sure. I have a strong feeling kissing a piece of cardboard isn't going to be nearly so satisfying as kissing you in person, though."

Even on the phone, Simon had the ability to excite her, and rouse her desire to see him, be with him. He talked the greatest nonsense for fifteen minutes, then told her he loved her and hung up. He hadn't said exactly when he would be in Brighton again, but as he had even spoken of hiring a house on Sunday, she assumed he would be there at least a few times a week.

She went to work on Tuesday morning humming a cheerful tune. She was surprised to see Jessie there in the morning.

"Emergency, darling," Jessie said. "I'm off to London. Gus says he'll excuse me from this afternoon's rehearsal. He's going to rehearse his play, the one I'm not in. I'll be back for tonight's performance."

"What are you going to London for?" Tillie asked, instantly suspicious. Her greater fear was not that Simon had invited Jessie, but that she was going uninvited to try her luck with him.

"The photo session Charles arranged for me with Lothar Burack—you remember. I told you about it."

"Yes, of course," she said, breathing a sigh of relief. "What are you wearing?"

"As little as possible. I'm taking a couple of outfits in my carryall. I'll let the great man decide."

"Is Charles going with you?"

"No, he's already there. He went down yesterday. I have to take the train. One day I will have my own car, Tillie, and a chauffeur to drive it. Every time I take a train or bus, I become more determined to be a star. I don't care *what* I have to do to make it. It's only the first years that are tough, then you're at the top, and you can be the one dishing it out, instead of taking it."

She had never seen Jessica so determined before. "Good luck with the pictures. I hope they turn out well."

"They will. I'm very photogenic." Several framed and unframed pictures of her that decorated the dressing room testified to the fact. She had even gotten herself blown up to poster size to cover the back of the door.

Jessie waved and left, and Tillie settled down to work. She went through *The Rivals,* revising her handwritten stage direction to take into account the new presentation. The day flew along happily. She went home to catch Simon's show at six on her television. The latter half of the program dealt with political corruption, a theme that was creeping more frequently into Simon's show now. He mentioned that Thursday night he would present a look at the Royal Pavilion in Brighton and the corrupt man who had built it. Tillie made a mental note to be sure to see the show, as she had been present when the idea was hatched.

She hurried back to the theater, worrying whether Jessie would be there in time for the show. If this Lothar Burack invited her to a party of celebrities, for instance, her professionalism would have hard work convincing her to decline.

She was there, eating a hamburger and chips from a brown paper bag. "How did the session go?" Tillie asked her.

"Smashing. He did me nude. Well, actually I had on a bikini, but he only did me from the bust up, so that I'll look nude, with my hair streaming over my shoulders. He says he perceives me as a sleek, sensuous cat. Isn't that sweet?"

"Sounds more like Lady Godiva to me. He should have given you a horse."

"Funny, that's just what Sim—Charles said."

"Charles or Simon?" Tillie asked quickly.

"Damn! He told me not to tell you. It was perfectly innocent, darling. All we did was *talk*. I phoned him. He told me to give him a call whenever I was in town, so I did."

"Did you see him?" Tillie asked.

"I had a couple of hours to kill before catching the train, and we went to a museum. *Really!* You don't have to look ready to scratch my eyes out, Tillie. We didn't spend the afternoon making love, as you seem to think. In fact, Simon is nutty over you. He talked about you all the time. Has he asked you to move in with him?"

"It's none of your business, but no, he hasn't."

"It wouldn't surprise me a bit if he did. He practically said as much. Lucky you! If you don't want him, pass him along."

"You can consider him yours. I'm not interested in moving in with Simon Cranston or anyone else. And you can tell him so the next time you phone him. You'll be talking to him before I am."

"I'll be very happy to give him the message. I expect to hear from him tomorrow, as it happens. Pass the salt, will you, darling?"

"Get it yourself," Tillie said, then marched angrily from the dressing room before she gave in to temptation and pulled Jessie's hair from her head. Show time was fast approaching, but she had to get out of the theater, away from Jessie. She ran down to the beach, to pace angrily to and fro over the shingle, nursing her poor treatment at Simon's hands. If he really loved her, he wouldn't have dropped all his work and gone running to spend a few hours with Jessie. That was painful enough to consider, but to know his intentions amounted to no more than sharing a roof for a few months was worse. He had been careful not to use the word *marriage*. She had noticed its absence on more than one occasion.

All he had ever had in mind was an affair, and she, like a fool, had transformed it into a true and lasting love, with church bells—even children. But Simon planned to have some solitude to write his book, and wanted someone to keep his bed warm and look after him in Cornwall. Never mind that there was no work for *her* there. What did *her* work matter to *him*? He was vain, selfish, egotistical—a male chauvinist pig—as she had known from the first time she met him. Of course he liked her better without makeup— what would a glamorous actress want with a poky cottage in the wilds?

A glance at her watch told her it was time to return to the theater. She didn't want to, but in the tradition of the theater, the show must go on. She was thankful for all the hours of rehearsal, drumming her role into her until it was second nature. The words said themselves. She didn't know whether she performed well, but at least she performed. She didn't let the troupe down. No one chided her for poor work afterward, so it must have been passable.

"Coming down to the pub?" Ron asked as the curtain descended after the last bow.

"Not tonight, thanks. I'm tired."

"How about you, Jess?" he continued.

"Beer is fattening, and you won't meet anyone who matters at Nick's Tavern," was her reply. "I have to make a phone call."

Tillie, despising herself for it, hung around Gus's office talking to Gus while Jessie made her call. Not till she heard her ask for Charles Greville did she go to the dressing room and change out of her costume. She hadn't accomplished much, either. Jessie would probably run right home and call Simon from her flat.

She rehearsed the scathing things she would say to Simon when he called that evening, taking for granted he would call. He didn't. It was to be another imperious ring at the last minute. I'm in town and will pick you up at . . . Not likely, Mr. Cranston. Not this time!

Her anger continued throughout the next day, making even her work difficult. There, at least, she had once found a haven from worry. Now she found concentration difficult, inspiration impossible. The rehearsal lagged. She went home early, and caught herself looking at her watch every five minutes, waiting for six o'clock, when she would see him, hear his voice.

She switched on the set and settled in to do some serious hating. It was impossible. He was too nice, too handsome, too lively and witty, too charming to hate as she wanted to. His show that evening was not one of the politically oriented pieces he had been doing lately. The theme was show business—her own favorite type of show.

He did an update interview with a sex-symbol-turned-authoress who had published her memoirs. The woman admitted that she had gained forty pounds, and said she loved every one of them. She was happy. She talked about the short life span of a sex symbol, urging starlets to have some other pan on the back burner for when their beauty faded. Tillie wondered if Jessie was watching and listening. Next he talked with an actress who stood at the height of her powers. She was doing a stage play, and had just finished a new movie. Having done the past and present, he said he would next feature the future. "Next year's blonde," he called her. "Miss Jessica Miter."

Tillie sat stunned, her eyes staring, unbelieving, at the screen. When had he done the interview? Why hadn't Jessie told her? They had conspired behind her back to do this. He showed a clip from the Brighton interview with Gus and Jessie, and another taken during a performance. It was Jessie's best scene, where she got to cry and rant and rave. This done, he turned to chat to Jessie in person. She was wearing the outfit she had worn to London the day before. Yes, that's when it was done, and Jessie saying they had gone to a museum! Her hair was different, but it wouldn't take her but two minutes to alter that.

The great surprise of the interview was that Jessie had won a role in an upcoming TV sitcom in January. This would be the role she had spoken of at Simon's party. She shared top billing with two other women— the three of them would-be actresses whose job-seeking antics were to be the plots for the series. He flirted with her; complimented her on her physical attributes; said he looked forward to seeing her on TV in the winter; and prophesied a meteoric rise to fame. Jessie was at the top of her form, answering so guilelessly that one wondered whether she was a simpleton, a very good actress, or—incredible thought—just plain telling the truth.

When the show was over, Tillie turned off the TV and sat looking at the blank screen, peopling it from her imagination. While she was in this dazed state, the phone rang. It was Gus, asking if she had seen it. Then Ron phoned, and a few others from the cast. They were all astonished, wondering if Jessie would finish out the summer with them or have to go to

London for rehearsals. They agreed it was Simon's influence that had landed her this plum, and wondered how they might bring themselves to his attention.

"And here I was beginning to think he was *your* fellow," Ron said innocently.

"No, he's not my type at all," she answered tartly.

"I don't know about *you*, but *I* intend to be very attentive to Jess for as long as she's with us. They're bound to need young guys for that series, don't you think?"

"Opportunist!" Tillie charged, but not angrily. The theater was a tough career. No possibility for a job was overlooked.

It was a dog-eat-dog world. Use your friends, and pay whatever price you have to, to get the break. There wasn't much doubt in her mind what price Jessie had paid Simon for this break.

At the theater, Jessica was in her element. If she wasn't a star yet, she was being treated like one. The local reporter was there, getting the story for the Brighton paper. With a subject like Jessie, pictures were not omitted, either. The cast gathered around her, hoping for a bit part in her series. Gus was happy for her, too. Any publicity that involved his cast was good for the show's business.

"Will you be able to finish the summer with us?" he asked, concerned over this important point. Such details as contracts did not exist yet with his group.

"Gus, darling, I'm a pro! Of course I'll finish the summer. We go into rehearsals in September, for January release."

She shooed them all out of the dressing room at the last minute, to prepare for the evening's performance. When they were alone, Tillie asked, "When was the interview done, Jess?"

"At the studio in London yesterday. Didn't Simon tell you?"

"I haven't spoken to him."

"That's funny. He told me not to tell you. He wanted to explain it himself, he said."

"That would be why you lied to me then?"

"It wasn't a lie, really. We *were* at a museum for a few minutes, on our way to the studio. I know what you're thinking, darling, but you're wrong. I just did Simon a little favor, and he did me a big one in return."

"You underestimate yourself, Jessie. I'm sure the favor you did him was a big one, too."

"Maybe it was. *He* seemed to think so anyway. I don't like to serve friends a dirty trick, but life is hard, darling. It's every woman for herself. I'm tired of being a pedestrian, remember?"

Tillie bristled silently, then changed the subject. "Would it be possible for me to have a corner of the mirror? I'm in this play too, in case you've forgotten."

"You're not in the first scene. I'll be through in a sec. You haven't congratulated me, Tillie."

"Congratulations."

"I might be able to help you—get you on as assistant director or something. Simon mentioned doing something for you, too."

"Simon doesn't owe *me* any favors. I haven't done him any. I'd rather advance my career on my two feet, thanks very much."

"What a nasty mind you have. Why, it's enough to give Simon a disgust of you, if he hasn't gotten one already. Funny he didn't bother to phone. I'll tell him tonight how angry you are. I'll be seeing him after the show."

"Charles is getting the gate again, is he?"

"Charles is conveniently in London. Perhaps you'd

be interested in looking him over, now that I have bigger fish to fry."

"I'm not interested in an alcoholic petty criminal."

"Petty? Oh no, Charles thinks big. There, I'm ready," she said, picking up the atomizer for her final touch of charm.

One short scene was not long enough for Tillie to compose her nerves. She was distracted during the show and her timing was off. Once she even forgot her lines, but Ron covered adroitly. As soon as the show was over, she fled home, not even bothering to change out of her stage costume and makeup, for fear of encountering Simon in the dressing room. She didn't want to see him, or be seen, in her upset state.

She decided to shower, and get all her washing done at once. She let the water pelt hard against her body, enjoying the sharp, stinging spray. She was in a mood for physical suffering, to match her lacerated emotions. She washed her hair too; then wrapped it in a towel, turban style; put on her robe; and came out of the room in her bare feet. The doorbell was ringing hard and repeatedly, as though someone had been ringing for a long time, and was impatient.

She thought it was Ron and the gang, going out to celebrate Jessie's triumph. They had seen the light in her flat and stopped. Except that the way to the pub did not lead past her flat. Could it be Simon? No, he was with Jessie. Maybe the gang was going to some fancier spot than Nick's tonight. This was a special occasion.

She opened the door to admit an impatient, angry Simon Cranston, his face set in a scowl. She tried to close the door against him, but he had his foot wedged in it, and soon pushed in past her.

"What the devil's going on here?" he demanded. "I've been trying to call you all day. Your phone was busy for an hour, then when I got to the theater, they said you'd left—"

"Are you sure it was *me* you were asking for? I understood it was Jessie who had a date with you tonight."

"I know what you're mad about. I wanted to tell you myself, before it went on the air, but I got tied up in production problems and couldn't get free in time. I called you the *instant* I could get away. Called you four or five times. I want to explain about Jessie."

"She has already explained about the little favor she did for you. You pay handsomely for ladies' favors, Simon."

"It wasn't that kind of a favor."

"What other kind could there possibly be between you and her? I know what she is, and I'm rapidly coming to realize what *you* are. You didn't get her that TV role for boiling you up a pot of her oily coffee. I didn't come down in the last rain, Simon. I've been around the business long enough to know the various routes to the top."

"If you'd stop ranting long enough, I'd tell you."

"I'm not interested in hearing any more of your lies. You don't want to keep her waiting. She's not as patient as I am."

"My date with Jessie is for midnight. That gives us over an hour."

"Midnight? If you think you're going to park yourself here till midnight when she's ready for you, you've got another think coming. I don't run a lounge, Mr. Cranston. Try The George."

"I'm beginning to wonder what it is you *do* run here. You obviously didn't expect to see *me* at your door. Who is it you *usually* meet in your dressing gown. Mr. Muscle?"

"That's right. I meet him in my dressing gown, if I

bother to put on anything at all," she shot back angrily, wanting to fan his jealousy, to hurt him if it was possible.

The blood rushed to his face. "You've changed your tune from the other night when you were a trembling virgin," he said, grabbing her wrists.

"You forget I *am* an actress. Playing the ingenue was good practice for me."

His face floated menacingly above her, wearing an angry scowl, while his eyes glinted. "You were *lying* to me then?"

"Tit for tat. You never bothered to tell *me* the truth."

"I haven't lied to you about anything. I came to fill in the few omissions."

"No, you didn't lie. I misunderstood."

"You knew how I felt about you, what my intentions were."

"Jessie was kind enough to clarify any misunderstanding I had. I know your plan for moving to the wilds of Cornwall to write your next book. I'm not interested in being your companion and washing your socks and cooking while the great man writes his magnum opus. Find yourself another chore girl. I have a career of my own to get on with. I'm not likely to find any plays to direct on the coast of Cornwall. You'd have to make a better offer than that. Sorry."

"What is the price for your favors?" he asked, his jaw tightening as he squeezed her wrists harder and harder.

"A starring role. You got Jessie cheap: a third of a series. But then you were only getting about a third of Jessie."

"You would accompany me to Cornwall as my mistress if I promised you a role in a series?"

"*Promised?* Don't make me laugh. Men's promises

are writ in water. I might *consider* it if I had a signed contract in my pocket."

"I thought you were different from the others," he said, his voice becoming lower.

"You must have thought me more stupid, at any rate. Ready to stop everything the minute you called, any hour of the day or night."

"My time isn't my own. I'm a busy man, with a career to pursue. I came to see you when I could."

"I'm busy, too. Am I expected to be flattered with your scanty attentions?"

"Lots of women would be. I didn't have to drive all the way to Brighton to get a woman, any woman. I came to see you because I thought you were . . . genuine," he said, selecting the last word carefully.

"I thought you were, too, but you're not. You're a phony. As phony as Charles Greville, and as vain and egotistical as a movie star. One woman isn't enough for you. You've got to sample them all."

"Did I sample *you* when I had the opportunity?"

"No, you found me resistible. The opportunity won't be repeated."

"We'll see about that," he said with a sneer. "I still have benefits to confer. You've just told me the price. I'll consider whether I think it's a good bargain."

She wrenched her wrists from his grasp, rubbing them back to circulation. "I'd have to give it serious consideration myself—whether even being the star of my own show is worth having *you* in my bed."

"You didn't seem to mind the other night!" he reminded her, his eyes blazing with anger. He pulled her into his arms and kissed her ruthlessly. She fought him off till she could fight no longer. The weakness invaded her head first, then her arms and body. Unable to escape, she gave herself up to the bitter-sweet prison of his arms. When he at last raised his head, she clung to him. He pushed her away, carelessly undid the belt of her robe.

"You don't mind if I take a look at what you're offering?" he asked in a hatefully haughty way. His eyes lingered over her bosoms, traveling down to her legs.

She pulled her robe closed. He twitched it open again, as if it were a suit on a rack. She turned on her heel and strode into the bathroom.

"Please lock the door when you leave," she said, then locked the bathroom door.

She heard the outer door slam, rattle on its hinges; then she sat on the edge of the tub, trembling with nervousness from the ordeal.

Chapter Nine

The summer that had begun like a golden dream turned suddenly to lead. Tillie's heart was heavy. She continued with her work, trying to retain her enthusiasm for it, but it became increasingly difficult. During the afternoons, there was Jessie bragging to everyone about her career. There were reporters and photographers interviewing her and taking her picture. Many afternoons Jessie arranged with Gus to be absent, for a dash to London. She had consultations with TV directors, scripts to read, costume fittings. Her life was a whirlwind, her only complaint that till she started working for TV, she could not afford a car.

The days were hard enough; the nights were intolerable. She knew Jessie and Simon were having an affair. Occasionally he would come to the theater to pick her up, and on the weekends, Jessie let it be known she was in London. She would rush madly for the train station after the Saturday performance with her weekend bag already packed.

When Simon would visit the dressing room she shared with Jessie she'd come in to find them with their heads together, talking, laughing, sometimes even embracing. She knew he did it to spite her. The hard glitter in his eyes told her so.

It was a Saturday, the second week after their fight, that she came in after the play to see Simon twisting a bottle of champagne in an ice bucket. There were two stemmed glasses on the table. Jessie was a few minutes behind her, chatting with someone backstage.

"Hello, Simon," she said, willing her voice to normalcy. "Having a celebration, I see. What's the occasion? Finally decided to go and write that great book, or is it someone's birthday?"

"No book and no birthday," he answered offhandedly.

"Perhaps an engagement?"

He glared. "Just a little surprise for Jess. She likes champagne."

"Who doesn't?" she said airily, picking up a tissue and cream to remove her makeup.

"Would you care to join us?" he asked, looking around the room for another glass. His eyes lighted on the paper cups in a container by the sink.

"No thanks. Drinking champagne from a paper cup would be like making love in a dirty bed. It would spoil it."

"I prefer clean linen myself," he answered, a muscle twitching in his jaw.

Jessie came into the room, ran to Simon and kissed him loudly on the cheek. "You darling! How did you know I was dying of thirst? I didn't think I'd get through the last act."

"You're always dying of thirst," he said fondly.

Tillie risked a glance at them, as they sounded so very absorbed in each other. When she noticed Simon was watching her, she quickly turned her head away. The phone on the table jangled raucously. Jessie had had her own private line installed to handle her calls. Tillie, closest to it, picked up the receiver. It was Charles, asking for Jessie.

"Tell him I'm not here," Jessie said.

"Maybe you'd better speak to him. He could come along with us tonight," Simon suggested. Tillie was startled at the idea that Simon would welcome a third party on their date. Jessie's next statement surprised her even further.

"He's been with us the last two times! Surely we can dispense with him tonight."

Simon considered this for a moment. He actually appeared *eager* for Charles's company! But in the end, Jessie had her way, and Tillie told Charles she wasn't in.

"Bother," Charles said on the line. "Here I have driven into town to meet her. I've ordered a very nice dinner for two at The George. I wonder—I don't suppose I could induce *you* to join me, Tillie?"

She had never cared for Charles in the least, but as she glanced at Simon and Jessie she knew she didn't want to go back alone to her apartment, either. She'd go with him for spite. The others would be drinking their champagne for half an hour. Let them see Charles call for her.

"It would be a shame to waste a nice dinner," she said. "Sure, Charles, I'd be happy to go."

"Wonderful. I'll pick you up in five minutes."

"Give me time to change. Make it ten," she countered.

She noticed Simon look toward her. He was frowning.

"I'm going out with Charles. You don't mind, Jess? I believe you said that you were through with him."

"Feel free," Jessie answered with a possessive hand on Simon's arm.

"You can't go out with him," Simon said firmly.

"Maybe she could find out—" Jessie said. Simon silenced her with a look.

"Why not? It's a free country, isn't it?" Tillie said casually.

"Because he's a lecher," he answered.

"Who isn't? We girls would sit home with a book every night if we waited around for Mr. Right."

She remembered that she had only her light cotton dress to change into. "Jess, could you lend me something to wear?" she asked. "We're having dinner at The George. I don't want to look too bucolic."

"Simon says you can't go," she pointed out uncertainly.

"Simon may have *you* under his thumb. Not me. I'm going. How about your black sun dress with the short jacket? You're not wearing it tonight, are you? You wore it Wednesday."

"It's too low-cut," Simon objected.

"Oh really, Papa!" she laughed, enjoying his jealousy. "I'm a big girl now. May I, Jess?"

"I guess so," she answered.

Tillie took the gown behind the screen that provided a modicum of privacy for changing. She hummed quietly as she undressed. The happy lovers beyond had sunk into silence. She would have a perfectly ghastly evening. Charles would drink too much and probably fall on his face before dinner was over, but at least she wouldn't have to wrestle with him in his car afterward. She'd take a cab home.

When she was dressed, she walked to the full-length mirror in the corner to examine herself. The gown was a little loose on top. Not many girls were as full above as Jessie, but at least it looked good enough to wear. She put on black patent sandals, also Jessie's. They looked much better on herself, she noted with satisfaction. Her calves tapered to a set of very trim ankles. In the reflection of the mirror, she saw Simon casting a long, sideways glance at them.

She walked over to the dressing-table mirror to put on fresh makeup in the better light. She carefully applied lipstick, a light touch of rouge. She brushed her long hair, humming all the while, to show Simon she was happy with her date.

"My glass is empty, Simon," Jessie said in a piqued tone.

He poured her another glass, but when he finished, his eyes again turned toward the mirror to watch Tillie fuss with her hair. He still looked very much as though he wished to object. Tillie ignored him, or pretended to. It was impossible not to be aware of him there while she performed her feminine toilette.

"Can I borrow a touch of your perfume?" she asked, when she was satisfied with her appearance. Without waiting for permission, she picked up the cut-glass bottle and squeezed the rubber ball, then looked at the label. "I see Night of Love is all gone. My Sin, this one is called. Hmmm, we'll see." She allowed a seductive little laugh to escape her lips. "How do I look?" she asked, turning around to face them. Simon looked like a baited animal, his eyes dark with frustration.

"Super. Doesn't she look nice, Simon?" Jessie said.

"It doesn't suit you," he answered curtly.

"Don't worry. It will suit Charles," Jessie said, laughing. "It suited him when I wore it. He'll probably recognize it."

"You'd better put on the jacket," Simon said

sharply. When she ignored him, he got the jacket and put it around her shoulders.

"It might be less embarrassing if Charles didn't see Simon and me here. Would you mind not bringing him in?" Jessie asked.

"Not at all."

There was a tap at the door. She removed the jacket, and with it hanging from one finger, went out to meet Charles, her hips swaying gently. She felt she had scored a small victory. Simon was definitely as angry as a hornet to see her going out with another man. It wasn't much, but it was something.

Charles was relatively sober. "Charming, Tillie," he said with a formal bow.

He wore a blazer and pale slacks. Charles usually wore a blazer. He had a range of them. This one was dark green, with a crested pocket.

"Très élégante," he added, offering her his arm.

He did not have romance on his mind. It was Jessie he wanted to talk about, which suited his companion fine. They went to a table already set for two. A bottle of wine was open, and half gone. Charles had interrupted his drinking to pick her up.

"It's a Chablis," he said. "I hope you like white wine. I've changed the order to lobster. I know you like it. You and Simon mentioned it."

"I love it."

"Jessie likes it too, but she can't eat it. It disagrees with her. I think a good strong constitution is inherited. The underbred have weak stomachs. Jessie's father is a dealer in secondhand merchandise, you know. Runs a hovel of a shop in Manchester. What is the world coming to, when a ragpicker's daughter spurns the advances of a Greville, an old family, a member of the Privy Council?"

Charles had certainly not changed. As much a snob as ever. "Jessie doesn't care much about that sort of thing."

"No. All *she* cares about is Jessie. She *used* me, Tillie. Used me badly, in my opinion. I got Lothar Burack, the famous photographer, to do her, but Simon Cranston has bigger plums to tempt her with. She drags him along on our dates as often as not, seeing what she can get out of him. She had the gall to ask permission to use my gate house for a party. I told her no, in pretty short terms. Cranston used to be your beau, I think?"

"Hardly that. Just an acquaintance."

"You're too good for him and I am too good for her. I noticed as soon as I met you, you were a cut above them. It doesn't do to go slumming. What does your father do?"

"He's a doctor, a general practitioner in Kent."

"Ah, a university man. I was correct about your background, then. There is nothing like breeding when you come down to it. I'd like to know Cranston's antecedents. He is careful not to mention them."

"His father is a farmer."

"A basket word. It sounds grand enough—one envisages rolling miles, dotted with cattle—but the fellow is probably a dirt farmer, eking a living out of a half acre. The fellow is a muckraker, you know. There isn't a member of the house who will give him the time of day."

She felt her temper rise at these slurs on Simon. Angry as she was with him, she felt a desire to defend him. "I thought you liked him, Charles."

"Liked him? Oh, he is amusing enough. He's been around the world a little and rubbed off the rough edges. He's learned to make himself acceptable to the upper classes. He passes for a gentleman among his own sort, I fancy. I suspect you'll not find a thing but common laborers in his whole family."

"There's nothing wrong with that. And if his background *is* poor, it's to his credit he rose above it."

"I think you still care a little for him. I grant you he has a handsome exterior. Mongrel dogs are often the most appealing—They have a certain liveliness. Jessie too has the mongrel charm."

That was the nature of their dinner conversation. Charles kept running Jessie down, but his comments showed clearly it was all sour grapes. Tillie had one glass of wine; Charles finished the bottle and ordered another with the dinner.

"Don't forget you have to drive home," she felt obliged to remind him.

"Not tonight, my dear. I have booked a room at the hotel. I had hoped Jessie—" He came to a stop, not yet drunk enough to utter the whole truth: that he had hoped to pass the night there with the ragpicker's daughter. "I shall see you home in a cab, of course. I am a gentleman."

She found him a pitiful gentleman, hanging on to his family's ancient glory. During the second bottle, he became maudlin. He told her of the military exploits of his ancestors, who had fought with Cromwell and with various Richards and Henrys and Georges. "My own father was a general," he added.

"Were you ever in the army, Charles?"

"Alas, no. Unborn for the First World War, and too young for the Second. Failed opportunities. A man can't be a hero nowadays. The lower orders have usurped our place. They would like to wipe out the distinction between the classes, and use taxes to accomplish it."

She became bored as he spoke again of the same

old complaints. He rambled on while she looked around the dining room. She was surprised to see Gus Brooks at a table, all dressed up and all alone. She waved to him, inviting him to join them, but he quietly shook his head in a negative. There was to be no rescue from the boring Charles.

When she returned her straying attention to him, he was saying, "When I die, Wespark will go for taxes. I haven't a son to leave it to, but I had hoped to have. Still hope, in fact. Soon I must marry and have a son and heir."

Further ramblings revealed it was Jessie he had selected for the role of mother. "She was beneath me, of course. What I ought to look for is a wellborn lady like you. Is there any distinction in your family?" he asked bluntly.

"My uncle was awarded the Order of the British Empire. Oh, and my great uncle was an admiral in the First War," she remembered.

"They are giving the OBE to anyone nowadays," he said sadly, too drunk to know he was being offensive. "Even young rock-and-roll guitar players. The monarchy is as bad as the commoners at this business of debasing society. Who does Princess Margaret marry? Nobody. It started with Edward the Eighth's marrying an American divorcée."

She glanced again to Gus, to see he was not eating dinner, but having coffee. She was happy it was not liquor, for he had been there for some time. After an hour and a half, she said, "I must be going now, Charles. Thank you so much for asking me."

"See you home . . . gentleman," he mumbled, his eyelids heavy.

"Why don't you just go up to your room, and I'll take a cab home."

It wasn't difficult to persuade him to this course of

action. Poor Charles, such a dreadful snob. With no accomplishments of his own, he had to deride everyone else's. She went to speak to Gus when Charles had been led upstairs by a waiter.

"What on earth are you doing here all alone?" she asked, her curiosity burning.

"Somebody had to look after you," he told her, smiling in an avuncular way. "I don't like to interfere in people's private lives, but that is really not fit company for a woman like you, Tillie."

"He's not fit company for anyone. What a bore. How did you know I was here?"

"Simon told me," he answered warily.

"Did he ask you to come and baby-sit me?"

"We agreed it was a good idea. He feels responsible, as he thrust you into the man's attention."

She sniffed, trying to be angry, but in truth was more gratified than otherwise. "Since you're here, you might as well give me a lift home."

"I intend to as soon as I finish my fifth cup of coffee. I'll hold you responsible for my sleepless night."

"You heard Ron is going to London for some tryouts for TV?" he asked as they drove to her flat.

"No. When did this happen?"

"Just today. I won't have either him or Jessie back with the company next year."

"This August is the end of the company, Gus, let's face it. It was a very short-lived company, but it's done everyone a lot of good. Who knows, your kids might be stars one day. And I *know* you are going to make a sensational comeback. Don't forget me when you need a spare hand with one tiny bit of experience."

"No, I won't forget you, Tillie, and that's a promise. I don't think he's having an easy time forgetting you, either. You know who I mean." It was not a question.

"Yes, I know who you mean."

"Can I do anything to help?"

"No. No thanks, Gus. See you tomorrow," she said, hopping out as soon as the car stopped. She just couldn't discuss Simon.

When she got to her apartment door, the phone was ringing. She ran to it, breathless. There was no fear, but rather an intuition that it was Simon. "Hello."

"I see you got home all right," Simon said.

"Yes, your baby-sitter drove me home. It wasn't necessary to check up on me. I had an enjoyable evening."

"Did Charles behave himself?"

"But of course. He is a gentleman," she said ironically. There was a silence from the other end. "Where are you calling from, Simon?" she asked.

"Jessie's place."

"Oh. Well, I'm home safe and sound and alone. You can relax."

"I could come over if—"

"That's not necessary. Thanks for calling. Bye." She put the receiver down quickly, an angry pulse beating in her throat. What must Jessie have made of that: Simon calling her and offering to come over. She had an image in her mind of Jessie tucked up in bed while Simon phoned from the kitchen—where he was making coffee after having made love.

While she still stood there thinking, the phone ran again. "What is it?" she asked angrily, knowing now who it would be.

"Are you busy tomorrow?" Simon asked—rather humbly, for him.

"Yes, I'm going to the beach with Ron and some other people."

"Ron?"

"Ron Beccles. Mr. Muscle to you."

"Where was he tonight when you needed him?"

"Out celebrating, I expect, and I didn't need him. I'm going to bed now. Please don't ring me up again tonight."

She wondered, after she had hung up for the second time, whether she had been a bit hard on Simon. She should have thanked him for his concern at least.

She went to the beach the next day with Ron and all the troupe. Her eyes kept looking down the long stretch of coast, thinking she might see Simon and Jessie. Wherever they spent the day, it was not at the beach. The beach, in fact, was nearly as boring as Charles Greville. Miles and miles of pebbles worn smooth, spotted with bathers and dogs and towels. But she knew that if that one man suddenly appeared amid the pebbles and bathers, boredom would vanish as quickly as the wave that broke at her feet. How long did it take to get over a broken heart? Was the rest of her life going to be like this—waiting for nothing?

On Monday, a new play opened, so in the afternoon they had a dress rehearsal. It was exciting enough to push Simon to the back of her mind for a few hours. When Jessie agreed to go out with the gang after the evening performance to celebrate, Tillie felt a sense of relief that she didn't have a date with Simon—accompanied by a little regret that she would not be seeing him, even from a distance. She had been cherishing some slim hope he would come down to preview the new play. Seeing him with Jessie was torture, but it was marginally better than not seeing him at all.

The play went well. The group was working as a team now, coming to know each other's dramatic quirks. A new production, of course, had a few ragged edges, but in the end it would be good. On this occasion, Gus Brooks went with them to Nick's. He sat at the table between Jessie and Tillie, talking theater.

"You'll have to change your mannerisms for TV, Jessie," he said. "The broad strokes that suit the stage won't go down well on the small screen. You need a more natural style. Remember, your audience will be a few yards from you, not twenty-five or thirty or forty. Think of yourself as a guest, entertaining them in their house."

"I'll be taking lessons as soon as our session here is over. Simon put me on to a really good coach in London. She charges an arm for private tuition, but the BBC might hire her to give classes to their new people."

"We're a lucky pair, to have ended up under the wing of Mother BBC," Gus said contentedly. "You haven't got a line on anything yet, Tillie?" he asked, turning to his other side.

"Nothing definite," she admitted, but in fact she had nothing, period. She had been dangerously careless in that respect. While the others had scrambled to find a spot here or there, she had been exerting all her effort toward directing *The Rivals* and worrying about Simon. What *would* she do?

"You should apply to the BBC as well," Gus advised. "They have so many irons in the fire, there's bound to be something for you. You might have to start out as a script girl, but eventually—"

"Script girl?" Jessie asked, offended. "It would take

forever to work her way up. What you should do is talk to Simon, Tillie. He could get you a good job. Look what he did for me."

"Simon would be less inclined to put himself to the bother for me," she answered stiffly.

Ron, at the other end of the table, called for a toast. They raised their glasses and drank. Then it was Gus's turn. He went to the head of the table to make his little speech of thanks and congratulation. He did not come back to his place when it was over, but sat with Ron and some of the men.

"I think Simon *would* get something for you if you asked him," Jessie said.

"I have no intention of asking him. Let's talk about something else."

"Don't be an idiot! Simon likes you. I mean he really likes you a lot. He talks about you half the time I'm with him."

"That's very bad taste on his part. I'm surprised he would be so ill-mannered." She had a vivid memory of Charles's spouting off about Jessie, and the reason she had held accountable for it. Was it possible Simon was smitten with her after all?

"I guess he can't help himself," Jessie explained. "I knew I wasn't making any headway with him, but last night I realized I had a lost cause on my hands. He was nearly *frantic* when you walked out with Charles. He didn't want to follow you himself, so he made poor Gus *promise* he wouldn't let you and Charles out of his sight. And then we went to my flat and he just sat there dialing your number, and hopping into his car every ten minutes to cruise past The George and your apartment, like a crazy man. What did you two fight about, anyway?"

"Let's change the subject. This is supposed to be a party."

"I hope it wasn't *me*," she persisted.

"I'm not as broadminded as you, Jess. I know you don't mind in the least if I see Charles; I can't seem to feel that way with Simon."

"We're just friends, Simon and I. I never thought I'd live to see the day I had to make such an admission. I didn't make it to first base with him. I did a favor for him, and he repaid me by speaking to the producer at the BBC. He didn't get me the job, exactly. He just introduced me to Ron Leduc, and I did the rest all by my little self. An opportunity—that's all he provided."

"It sounded like more than friendship when he interviewed you on his show."

"Oh sure, that's to make the show amusing. Simon doesn't consider the show so much educational as entertainment. It's an act."

"What was this little favor you did him, then?"

"I can't tell, but if you think it was—you know—sex . . . well, you're wrong. He wouldn't have to pay for that, Tillie. The pretty young things are lined up waiting for a chance at him. You should see them at the studio. It shocked *me*, and I thought *I* knew a thing or two about getting a man."

"Can't we talk about something else now? Who is this woman who's going to coach you?"

"Her name is Ida Letterman."

"I've heard of her. She's supposed to be very good."

"She's the best. But, Tillie, we're not finished with the other topic yet. I can't talk here. Come back to my flat after the party, and I'll tell you. Simon said not to, but I will."

After this intriguing statement, the party seemed interminable. The others were still at it when the two women left. Jessie had a flat similar to Tillie's own Spartan place, except that it was much messier.

"Simon can't *believe* the way I live," Jessie laughed. "I tried to blame it on the cramped quarters, but he insisted that *Tillie's* place didn't look like a rat's nest, and it was no bigger than mine. Of course, you don't have umpteen dozen outfits to stow in a fifteen-inch-wide closet. Want some coffee?"

"Sure. I have a feeling I won't be doing much sleeping tonight in any case."

They talked about minor matters till the coffee was readied and served up in two coarse, thick mugs, one without a handle. Tillie wondered what Simon had thought of that.

"You were going to tell me about you and Simon," Tillie reminded her.

"Me and Charles and Simon," Tillie corrected. "It was never me he wanted to meet. It was Charles. I just happened to be a good friend of Charles. Simon says Charles is involved in some bribery having to do with government paving contracts. He took a kickback to give the contract to a friend, or a fellow crook or something. The contract came in at a stiff price, but Charles explained that he wanted a really good job done, so he paid the higher price. It was a lousy job, of course, as the broken surface on our local roads will show. The contractor did a cheap job, and half the excess profits went into Charles's pockets. And of course, it's not only one road we're talking about. It's everything."

"Everything?"

"Different things. Charles is a kind of advisor on financial matters in the government. You know he travels around a lot, arranging sales and purchases of government supplies. Plenty of chances for payola, as long as he has a venal party at the other end. It could be *millions* of pounds we're talking about. I mean, when you get into armaments and things like that, the figures are big. This is not just a little local scandal, Tillie, it's big-time stealing. That's why Simon didn't want you to have anything to do with Charles. He wouldn't even let me do any gentle quizzing, in case Charles tumbled to what I was up to. Charles got rather snifty with me, toward the end."

"He mentioned not letting you use his gate house for some party. Had that anything to do with Simon?"

"Simon took the notion Charles had his money hidden there, but he hasn't. Simon sneaked in while Charles was in London and went over it with a fine-tooth comb. What Simon is trying to do is find out if Charles has already got the money smuggled into a Swiss account, or if he has just bought something portable with it. Oil paintings he thought a possibility. Charles thinks he knows something about art, you know."

"So that's why he was urging Charles on to drink at Wespark?"

"Charles never needs much urging. It was perfectly clear from his life-style he spends more than he makes. That's why Simon wanted to meet him on a personal basis; get him talking, you know, to see if he could find out anything. He's such an awful braggart he can't keep things to himself. His career is about finished. He's practically ostracized from the government right now, and once he is retired and skips with his loot, there'll be no catching him."

"He talks pretty freely when he's been drinking."

"Not toward the end. I think he tumbled to it that Simon was after him. He was rather suspicious at Simon's joining us on our dates so often, after I arranged the introduction at the Beefeater. In the end we couldn't get a thing from him."

"I notice it didn't stop Simon from seeing you, though."

"Darling, don't be ridiculous! What better excuse could he find to hang around the theater to see you? And if he could make you a little jealous in the bargain, so much the better. He's a pet. I call him when I have to go up to London. He lets me use his apartment to wait for buses and trains and things. Sometimes he's there, and sometimes he isn't. It's a gorgeous place. When I'm rich, I'll have something like it. He has a dark green tub as big as a bathing pool, with gold-colored faucets, though they're only brass. He wouldn't let me have a bath."

"Did you ask him?"

"Of course. I was dying to try it. It has a Jacuzzi. It helps him to relax after a hard day."

"You're incorrigible. So what happened about Charles and the bribery? You didn't find any proof—anything that could be used as evidence?"

"Nothing. He's guilty, but without finding the money or proof of where the money was spent, Simon's hands are tied. Innocent till *proven* guilty, you know."

"What we've got to do is find out what Charles did with the money, then."

"Impossible. Charles doesn't trust me."

"He still loves you."

"He loves Charles. He *desires* me, but he never asked me to marry him. Except when he's drunk, of course. Then he chats about it, but when he's stone cold sober, he wouldn't *dream* of it. I'm not high enough in society to suit him. He'd like to make me his permanent mistress, I think. He has grandiose and antiquated ideas about living in the ancient style. And anyway, what would I want to marry that old crook for? I have my career. Simon got me the opportunity, and it's up to me to do something with it. Did I tell you *Playboy* wants me to pose?"

"No, you didn't," Tillie answered absently. Her mind was veering off in another direction. Charles didn't trust Jessie, but he trusted her. He had approved of her gentility, her university-trained father, her admiral uncle. Maybe he'd ask her out again. . . .

"So why don't you pick up that phone and call Simon?" Jessie asked, pointing to the phone sitting on the floor—there being no other surface clear to hold it.

"It's too late, and besides, I don't like to phone men."

"Oh really, darling, this *is* the twentieth century."

"Yes, I don't suppose many women phoned men before the telephone was invented. Jessie, you mentioned something once. . . . You said Simon wanted to live with me. Did he say that?"

"He indicated it. I can use my eyes."

"You said *live*, not marry."

"I repeat, it is the twentieth century. You've spent the night with Ron. Wouldn't you prefer Simon?"

"I have not! Where did you get that idea? Did Ron say so?" she demanded angrily.

"No, Simon. . . . He came here one night, foaming at the mouth with rage. He didn't actually *say* it, but— You mean you haven't?"

"Oh Lord, what have I done? I was so mad at him I let on Ron and I were lovers, just to annoy him."

"It succeeded, darling. So he let on he was fond of me, to annoy *you*, and of course to give him an excuse to hang about Brighton. Shall I straighten out this little lovers' knot for you? It won't be hard for him to believe, since I've already indicated my astonishment that you and Ron were anything but friends. Who knows? He might even *marry* you. He has expressed a terrible disgust with the morals of the young since you told him that whopper."

"I want to think this whole thing over carefully. Don't say anything to Simon—not yet. If he doesn't call me, we'll see what has to be done. Look at the hour! I'm for home and bed."

"You can stay here if you like," Jessie offered. After a look through the open bedroom door, at a tangled mass of sheets, blankets and pillows, half of them trailing on the floor, Tillie politely declined.

"I'll have maid service too when I'm rich. See you tomorrow afternoon," Jessie said, yawning and stretching and looking suddenly very endearing to her former rival.

Chapter Ten

Tillie knew she had been foolish in her handling of the Simon affair. She set about to rectify her mistake. She would, in some as yet undertermined manner, discover where Charles had his money concealed. And if he had bought something with the money, she would find that out instead. She would impress Simon with her intelligence and daring. She would help him solve this matter, and he would be eternally grateful. The eternity would be spent within the bonds of a pair of golden rings.

The important detail to arrange was meeting Charles again. She must let him drink himself into revelation. Since he didn't distrust her, he might be less discreet than he was with Jessie. He seemed to like her, on the one date she had had with him.

On Tuesday, she sat looking at the phone, wondering if she should call Charles and invite him to come to the new play. She disliked phoning a man, but one in whom she had no real interest was easier to call than one like Simon. Twice her hand got as far as the receiver, only to be snatched back again in the hope that he would call her. Her reluctance paid off. Charles called the theater at seven, before the performance. He did not even ask for Jessie, but invited Tillie to go out afterward for a nightcap.

"What a splendid idea. I'd love it," she answered warmly.

"Good. I'll pick you up at the theater."

"I'll be waiting," she said, and put the receiver back, her hand trembling with fright and anticipation but her resolve firm.

"Was it Simon?" Jessie asked, looking an arch smile at her.

"No. Charles. I'm going out with him after the show."

"Oh Tillie, I wish you wouldn't. Simon won't like it."

"He'll like it if I can find out what he's done with the money."

"He'll never tell you."

"Don't be so sure. Blondes aren't the only women he likes."

"I know that."

"Did you know he thinks that I would make a suitably genteel mama for his son and heir?"

"Oh dear, he must have been completely drunk!"

"That's not much of a compliment. Anyway, it seems to me a prospective bride can hint for what size bank account her groom has hidden away, and I do mean hidden."

"Be careful, darling. Charles is not a complete fool, you know. He might put two and two together, remembering you were seeing Simon before I was."

"He remembers that, and has congratulated me on my taste in turning him off. I shall be the soul of discretion," Tillie promised.

Jessie frowned, dissatisfied with the twist things had taken. Maybe she ought to call Simon. When Tillie left the room for a moment, she phoned his apartment, but there was no answer. He must be still at the studio. The studio gave her a busy signal. Then Tillie came back and the call was forgotten.

Charles Greville, bored with his evening, decided to go and see the new play, which left him as sober as a judge and as dry as a bone when he picked up Tillie afterward.

"Are you in the mood for a spot of dinner?" he asked politely.

"To tell the truth, I'm too tired to eat, but I could do with a drink," she answered as he took her elbow to lead her to his car.

"If you'd care to drive out to Wespark with me, you could sample my absinthe," he mentioned offhandedly. She had a firm idea it was not the absinthe but the privacy he was after, and reacted accordingly.

"I prefer Pimm's, Charles. They have it right at The George—so much closer—and I *am* thirsty. All that talking onstage."

"A gentleman never says No to a lady when he can help it," he answered obligingly, turning the car toward The George. The car was handed over to the attendant while she and Charles went into the bar. There was a good crowd, enough to lend Tillie a feeling of safety. They sat at a small corner table, and he ordered drinks. The first drink he had was a double Scotch, which seemed like a clear indication of his seriousness in drinking.

* * *

He remained completely sober during his first two doubles, as Tillie slowly sipped her single drink. It was not till he was on his third that he began to wander into indiscretion.

"I wish you weren't an actress," he said.

"Why is that, Charles?"

"They are a trifle *déclassée*. Well enough for a mistress, but a gentleman wouldn't marry one."

"Plenty of gentlemen have. There was quite a rush on them during the Edwardian period."

"*Should* not marry one, is what I meant."

"I'm not really an actress. Directing is my true love. I'm just acting to get some theatrical experience."

"Directing, eh? That's very . . . modern of you. The gels today all want to work for a year or two before they marry. I am not stuck in the past. A man must move with the times. I don't mind a young lady having a career, so long as she straightens out when she marries. Why, even Lady Diana had a job. Taught at some school or other."

"It helps to pay the bills."

"I expect your family could afford to support you."

"Papa complains a great deal about the taxes, and the national health plan that limits his fees."

"Typical of the government," he said quickly, mindless of the fact that it was his government. "A man who can bank a pound a week is fortunate."

"It makes it difficult for couples to save up and get married," she pointed out.

"It makes it demmed near impossible. We have too much government. What the country needs is a benevolent dictator. Oh, I don't mean a Hitler, but some less violent sort of fellow. Still, there's no denying Hitler pulled Germany up by her bootstraps."

"And pulled it down again, along with the rest of Europe," she pointed out.

"Well, I am no Hitler-lover. He hadn't the proper respect for the past. The Bolsheviks the same, wiping out the good old families."

"It's really a shame to see the grand old estates like yours being parceled off," she lamented.

While Charles drank his way through the third double and ordered a fourth, Tillie continued to guide the meandering talk along the lines of excessive taxation, the necessity of a man's storing away a little something for himself. He moved closer to her, held on to one hand, and made a few attempts at lovemaking. As he finished his fourth, he was sufficiently drunk to begin imagining he wanted to marry her, and she was still sober enough to encourage him along that line.

"It sounds lovely, but what would we live on, Charles?"

"Ha. Don't worry your pretty little head about that, my dear. Old Charles is not stupid. He has managed to squirrel a little something away where the government can't find it."

"You sly fox! How did you do it?"

"Carefully. Very carefully," he said, and laughed inanely.

"Yes, but *how?* Aren't you afraid of getting caught?"

"It would take a smarter man than Mr. Simon Cranston to catch me. That's what he is up to, you know. A common fellow, common as dirt. The other members in London warned me away from him. Muckraker. You were wise to dump him. He has no respect for his betters. Jessie the same, preferring *him* to *me*. Let them go off together. We'll show them, eh Tillie?"

"You'll show them. I must confess I don't know what you're talking about."

"Jessie is an open book. I knew why she suddenly wanted to use my gate house. She knew I used to keep some things there."

"What things?" Tillie asked casually.

"No matter—just things. Artistic things, pictures . . . I sold them. Too bulky by half. There was nothing in the gate house, but I refused to let her inside. So she'd tell Simon that's where they were."

"You are clever," she praised, smiling fatuously on him. "Where *did* you put them?" she asked brightly, wondering what he was talking about.

"I won't tell you, but I'll show you if you come out to Wespark with me," he promised wih a smug smile.

"It's so late. How would I get home?" She was very loath to leave the safety of the inn.

"I'd drive you. I'm a gentleman. I'm offering you my hand in marriage, my dear. We'll celebrate our engagement at my home—a very private celebration," he added in meaningful accents. She feared his notion of a celebration involved the bedroom, but he was in no condition to do her any real harm. She could outrun him, or even outfight him.

"I'll go with you, then. But you must let me drive," she bargained.

"I'll buy you a car for a wedding gift. Any car you want, Jessie," he said, his mind so fogged he thought the brunette before him was the blonde he really preferred. "You've hinted often enough, eh?"

She felt a perfect fool, guiding his staggering steps out of the bar. The doorman assisted him into the car while she got behind the wheel and figured out how to get the car into motion. Her heart pounded with fright and excitement as they sped along the dark ribbon of road toward Wespark. She'd find out what he had squirreled and then she would leave—sneak out. She'd say she had to go to the washroom, and run to the car and drive home. She'd call Simon, and have him come and call the police. Charles would be sleeping it off at that point, and wouldn't be able to hide his ill-gotten gains.

The drive had the undesirable effect of sobering Charles somewhat. He opened the window and breathed in the cool night air. He also sat much too close for comfort, or even safety, but eventually she found the curved drive off from the main road and swept up to the front of Wespark. When she turned off the motor, Charles was sober enough to ask for the keys. She noticed he put them in the pocket of his trousers, which could be a difficulty if he didn't actually pass out stone cold.

There was no servant in evidence as they went through the dimly lit hall toward his private living quarters. Even before sitting down or offering her a seat, he said, "A nightcap?"

"Do you have any sherry?" she asked, accepting a drink to lull his suspicions, but making it a weak one to keep her own head straight. She had been obliged, over the long evening, to have two Pimm's es. Only one couldn't be stretched over nearly two hours. She was ravenously hungry, but didn't want to ask for food, in case it should make Charles sober.

He poured her sherry; a brandy for himself; and settled down on the sofa for a chat. She was afraid to mention wanting to see what he had promised to show her till he had had a few more drinks. He had a great tolerance for alcohol, indicating a prolonged drinking history. She knew she would be flat on her back if she had drunk half of his night's intake.

After one brandy, he became amorous. "Sit closer to me, my dear," he coaxed. She moved closer, felt his arm go around her shoulder. The next thing she knew, he was kissing her, suffocating her with his brandy-soaked lips. It was disgusting. The only way she could endure it was to remember that she was helping Simon. She let him kiss her twice, but when his hands began to explore her body, she suggested another drink.

"The little lady wants to get into the proper mood, I see," he answered pleasantly.

"I'll get it myself," she offered, to escape his arms. She took up his glass too, and filled it.

This done, there was nothing for it but to return to the sofa, where she was soon in his arms again. She could not imagine how Jessie had put up with him. His attempts at lovemaking were interrupted for a sip of the drink as often as she dared. She took minimal tastes, often nothing at all, while Charles continued to imbibe freely. At last his talk became maudlin enough that she dared to broach the subject that had brought her here.

"A honeymoon in Greece. How does that strike you, my dear?" he asked, smiling dazedly.

"It sounds perfect, but what will we use for money?"

"Money? We'll use the international currency."

"You mean gold?" she asked with interest, thinking this was what he meant to show her.

"Gold? I wish I had bought it before it soared. But gold is too heavy to smuggle out of the country. I mean diamonds," he said sagely, nodding his head.

"Oh Charles! Have you really got diamonds? I adore diamonds. May I see them?"

He looked at her for a moment, his eyes narrowing in suspicion. She smiled brightly. "Do you think I could keep one, just a tiny one, for an engagement ring?"

He relaxed into a smile. "You women are all alike. Of course you shall have one. You shall choose one, and it need not be a small one, either. I'll get them now, and let you make your choice."

She drew a deep, careful breath and held it as he wobbled to his feet to get his treasure. He did not even leave the room. He went to another sofa and picked up a cushion. It was a yellow velvet cushion, one of several that lay against the back of the sofa. "Jessie calls this my teddy bear, as I am so fond of it," he said.

Oh dear, he's too drunk! He has forgotten what he's supposed to be doing, she thought, deeply vexed. He began to unzip the outer covering, plunged his fingers into the densely packed goose feathers, and drew out a brown leather bag tied with a leather thong. It was not so very large, about four inches square. He loosened the draw, and a cascade of diamonds flowed into his outstretched hand. They caught the light from the lamps as they ran like water from the bag. Fleeting prisms of multicolored light flickered briefly, beautifully.

She arose and went to look at them more closely. They were of various sizes and shapes, some no larger than an apple seed, some closer to the size of a pea, and some twice again as large. Standing out in the pile were three large, perfect stones as big as plum pits. All were faceted, gathering up and reflecting the light as they were sifted to and fro in Charles's palm as he admired them.

"How lovely! Where did you get them?" she asked.

"In Amsterdam. I sold all my paintings from the gate house and took the money to Holland on my last trip. I brought them home in my briefcase, in a brown manila envelope marked 'private and confidential.' They didn't dare open the briefcase of a member of the Privy Council," he added haughtily.

"They must have cost a fortune."

"That needn't worry you."

"Shall I make my selection now?" she asked, continuing the charade.

"I know which one it will be," he nodded fondly, selecting the largest and handing it to her.

She accepted it, gave him a peck on the cheek, and offered a few words of compliment. Her aim now was to get him unconscious as quickly as possible so that she could get the keys and leave. At the very worst, if Charles sobered up enough to hide the others by the time Simon and the police came, she had this one piece of evidence.

Charles explained its pear shape, the exquisite faceting—done by the best diamond-cutters in Holland.

"I thought the best ones had left Holland after the war. Didn't you say so before?" she asked.

"I may have done. I did not want certain parties getting the notion I was too knowledgeable, or interested, in the business. Didn't completely trust Cranston."

"I'll put it in my change purse to make sure it gets home safely," she said when they had both finished admiring it.

"It will be better if I keep it here for safekeeping," he told her, removing it from her fingers.

"I'll take very good care of it. Don't worry I would lose it," she said earnestly.

"It must be mounted. We shall want to have it put into an engagement ring. I'll attend to it, my dear, and return it to you later."

As she stood trying to think of a good excuse to keep it, he slid the diamonds back into the brown leather bag; pulled the draw; and inserted the leather bag amid the goose feathers and did up the zipper. Very well then, she must suggest yet another drink.

"This calls for a toast," she declared.

"Absolutely!" he agreed, reaching for his glass. "To many happy years, and at least two sons."

"What, no daughters?" she asked, taking an infinitely small sip.

"First, a wife does her duty in supplying her lord and master a son or two, then she may have what she likes. You know what happens to wives who fail— Look at Josephine. Napoleon had to be rid of her. Henry the Eighth the same. He wouldn't be known as the beheading monarch if his wives had done their duty by him."

"What high company you put yourself in," she said, smiling to humor him along.

"I consider myself quite as high as that Corsican adventurer, at least," he replied, showing some signs of umbrage.

She made placating sounds. He moved closer to her and wrapped his arms around her. The next mood to overtake him was, unfortunately, desire. She submitted to his embrace, but when his hands groped clumsily for her bodice, she could stand no more. She pushed him off, as gently as her revulsion allowed.

"Now, Charles, we're not married yet," she said.

"Do you think I can wait that long for you?" he asked, his voice growing husky. She struggled against him, but was easily overpowered. She was thrown on her back on the sofa as he wrenched the top of her gown open. Two buttons pulled off and rolled on the carpet. The others opened more freely. She was seized by panic. The cold sweat stood out on her brow. As she struggled against him, she shouted for help. Surely some of the servants were in the house!

"Save your breath. You'll need it," he advised. "There's no one home to hear you. I only went into Brighton this evening because the servants weren't home to fix my meal."

His mood became uglier as he saw she was repelled by him. He struggled, trying to get on top of her. At last he got hold of her two wrists in one hand and held her down. He was gasping with the effort, his face so dark a red as to verge on purple. It seemed to take most of his strength. He won't be able to get undressed, she thought. He's old and drunk. I'm young and sober. I'll fight till he drops from exhaustion. She continued wrestling against his strength for what seemed an eternity, while all manner of fears and futile plans went through her head. Charles seemed to be enjoying the tussle.

He murmured approval of her spirit. "Hellcat," he gasped. "You have more fire than I hoped for. It will be a pleasure to tame you."

"Stop! Stop it! I'm not going to marry you. You can't do this."

The gloating laugh became uglier. "Do you think I really intended to marry *you,* a commoner? Father a country sawbones! My ancestors were feudal lords. I'll have you, strumpet, but not in marriage."

Her muscles were sore, wearied from struggling. She had been a fool to come. She gasped, and knew her strength was nearly gone. "Please," she said, her voice a whisper.

"That's more like it!"

"Please, don't," she gasped.

One hand came up quickly and struck the side of her cheek, sending her head off the edge of the sofa as he crouched above her on his knees. It caught her on the ears as well as the face, causing a ringing sensation. Surely it was that, and not— Could it *possibly* be the sound of stealthy movement in the hallway?

With her last gasp she opened her mouth and called, "Help! Help me!"

A sound of pounding feet sent Charles's head up, his eyes turning in angry horror to the doorway. He was still stradding Tillie on the sofa when Simon appeared in the doorway. It seemed impossible that a human being could move as swiftly as Simon moved to the sofa. He was like a man shot out of a cannon. He hauled Charles up by the collar of his jacket and one arm. He snarled an extremely uncouth expression as his right fist pulled back, and then slammed forward with great force, striking Charles on the chin. It took only one blow to drop him. He crumpled to the floor, against the side of the sofa. Simon gave him a push that sent him to the ground.

Simon turned his eyes, still wrathful, to Tillie. He looked angry enough to strike her too, till he saw her dazed, mauled condition: her dress half torn off, a red bruise on her cheek, her eyes wet, her expression wild.

He went down on one knee and enfolded her in his arms, with her head on his shoulder, murmuring soft words of reassurance. She closed her eyes and sighed in relief. It was so warm and safe and comfortable in his arms, listening to his worried, soothing voice. An uncontrollable shudder shook her when she realized how narrowly she had escaped. His arms held her more tightly, till she was calmed by the knowledge that the nightmare was over.

She became aware of other presences in the room: people looking at Charles and asking each other in low tones what they should do. It was Gus Brooks,

Jessie, and Ron Beccles. What were they all doing here? It didn't matter. They were here, her friends, and she was safe. She was in Simon's arms, held so tightly she could hardly breathe. She didn't care much about that detail.

"Give her your jacket, Gus," Simon called.

He put Gus's coat around her shoulders and buttoned a button to hide her torn gown. "Better call the police," was his next suggestion.

"I already did," Jessie answered.

"Simon, I found out what he did with the money," Tillie said when she had regained her breath.

"Hush. Later," he said, stroking her hair.

"I'm all right now. Really I am. He has a bag of diamonds in that yellow velvet cushion. He was going to run off to Greece. All that talk of Swiss bank accounts and Ireland was just a smoke screen."

"This cushion?" Jessie asked, picking up his favorite one. "No wonder he liked to have it near him! I've had it in my hands many times. Imagine, and I never knew!"

Simon twitched with interest, but in the end remained where he was, at her side, while Jessie unzipped the cushion and extracted the leather bag to show the others.

"Aren't you proud of me?" Tillie asked Simon.

"Proud? I'd like to break your gorgeous neck. How *dare* you come here alone with him? Have you no common sense? You're no more able to handle a lecher like him than—than I'm able to handle you."

"I was sure he'd pass out from drinking, but he didn't. He just kept drinking and drinking for hours."

"Are you all right?"

"Oh yes, I'm all right now," she said peacefully. Simon had a drink of Charles's Scotch, and Jessie made a pot of his coffee for the others. While they awaited the arrival of the police, Tillie outlined her story briefly. Charles had at last succumbed to the alcohol. He lay on the floor throughout the remainder of the interval, giving an occasional grunt but not opening his eyes.

When the police arrived, Simon had the facts straight, and told the story from its beginning—with his own interest in the London rumors that Charles was bribing public employees—to its end, with the handing over of the bag of diamonds.

"You'll have to come down to the office and sign a statement," the officer told them.

"Tomorrow. I'm taking the young lady home now," Simon replied.

"Oh, aye, I meant tomorrow. I'll just take the honorable member along to the lockup tonight, if one of you lads would be kind enough to get hold of his feet while I hoist up his shoulders."

Ron took the feet; Gus Brooks held the door for them, shut off the lights and locked the door behind them all.

"I'm staying with you tonight. I don't want you to be alone after this ordeal," Simon told Tillie when they reached her door. "I can sleep on the sofa."

"All right. I won't argue. I'm too nervous. How did you know I was there?" she asked, her mind settling down to rational thought when she entered her own familiar surroundings.

"Jessie called me at the studio to tell me what you were up to. She had the devil of a time reaching me; that's what made me so late. I tore down to Brighton at ninety miles an hour. In fact, I got a speeding ticket. I should make you pay it. I met the others at the theater, and we went looking for you. Jess suggested The George, and when you weren't there, we drove straight to Wespark. How did you come to do such a dangerous harebrained thing?"

"How else were you ever going to find out where he had hidden the money?"

"I would rather *never* have found out than to subject you to that. Jessie could have found out for me by that means. I wouldn't let *her* do it; you may imagine how likely it was I would let *you.*"

"*Let* me? I am not in your power, Simon. You couldn't prevent me. And furthermore, I don't think he would have told Jessie. He suspected her."

"Sit down. I'm going to make us some coffee."

She sat, not because he told her to, but because she was too exhausted to stand.

"He's really horrid," she said when he returned from the kitchen. "He asked me to marry him, then let out he had no intention of going through with it. It was just a ruse to get me . . ."

"You must have been persuasive to have coaxed a proposal from him! I trust we won't be hearing wedding bells."

"Of course not. I just wanted an excuse to quiz him about money. Being a fiancée gives a girl that privilege, you know."

"Quiz away," he said, taking her fingers and giving her a tired, arch smile. "In fact, I'll bring my accountant down to go over the books with you. I *did* tell you we're getting married, didn't I?"

"No, you haven't *asked* me, actually," she replied.

"You have to. You owe it to me. I have been at great pains to rearrange my life so that I can write my book in London. I have convinced my unwilling psyche that a cottage in the country is a state of mind. We'll plant a few tubs of corn or potatoes on the balcony of my flat. In that way, you'll be able to try your hand at directing, and I'll be available for some special TV documentaries old Mother BBC has in mind for me. It will be a diversion from writing, when the mood strikes me. The weekly show is finishing the last of August. That will put us both free in September. There is something nostalgic in an autumn wedding, don't you think?"

"I always wanted to be a June bride," she replied with studied mulishness.

"Pity we hadn't met in April, and I would have been happy to oblige you."

"It's unlikely we'd ever have met at all, when you consider it," she said. "If you hadn't happened to come down to interview Gus, and heard about Charles, we never would have."

"You have the wrong order. I was hot on the trail of the honorable member, and needed an innocent-appearing excuse to be often in Brighton, in the hope of striking up an acquaintance with him. So I looked around and happened to find out about Gus's dramatic venture. It gave me a good excuse to return and return."

"So that's why you kept coming! You let on it was to see *me!*"

"I had a double reason after I met you, either one of which would have been sufficient in itself. My employer, however, is a little tacky about romance. They wouldn't have let me do a whole series on Gus if they hadn't been given to understand my *real* motive was to track Charles down to his pot of gold."

"You'll be the golden-haired boy now, I expect?"

"Yes, this year's blond, you might say. They'll probably even let my wife direct a few shows."

"I don't plan to get ahead that way!"

"It's more like a toe in the door. You will meet the right people, at least. An opportunity is all I'm suggesting."

"Well," she said with careful deliberation, "I suppose there's no harm in seizing an opportunity. Maybe I could be somebody's assistant for a while. Larry Moss—"

"No!"

"Why not? He's safely married."

"Larry is a bachelor."

"You said he had three bouncing baby boys."

"I also said *you* were a kleptomaniac, as an insurance policy. I didn't want him getting in my way."

"That's dishonest."

"All's fair in love and war."

"Going out with Jessie wasn't fair—hanging around the dressing room, kissing her more than once."

"How else was I to keep an eye on you, and make you jealous? I wanted to beat you the night you first went out with Charles. You only did it to scare me, didn't you?"

"No, of course not. I did it to make you jealous, idiot."

"It wasn't necessary. I was already so jealous of Mr. Muscle I was losing sleep. My teeth took to aching on me. I couldn't concentrate on anything. I hoped I was cured the night you implied you were a scarlet woman, till some discreet questioning of Jess assured me you were a very innocent. 'A blushing violet who sneaks behind the screen to change her belt' was the delightful description she gave me. It was balm to my battered spirit. I had despaired of finding a woman like you, Tillie. You meet all kinds in my business, but outside of fairy tales, I hadn't had the fortune to find one like you."

"So you just made do with the other sort?"

"Opposites attract, they say. And the legions of 'other sorts' are a gross exaggeration. I passed up a good many more opportunities than I took, where women are concerned. Even you, dear heart, must confess I didn't take advantage of your inebriated state and I planned to *marry* you."

"You never said so. . . . Asked me, I mean," she added quickly when his smile stretched into a grin.

"I've told you now. And you're not drunk tonight, either," he added, reaching to pull her into his arms.

She gave herself up to him, secure now in the knowledge that he was serious. She thought she had no strength left in her after her exertions but felt a new force rise up to meet his ardor. It swelled like a tide when he lowered her onto the sofa and lay beside her without even loosening his grip.

They embraced passionately, but when he moved to touch her breasts, he stopped and pulled his hands away. He placed them on her warm neck instead, his fingers just reaching to her collarbone. She put her hands around his neck to pull him back to her, enticing him with a kiss. His hands moved slowly across her body, gently down around her waist.

"Simon, it's all right. We're getting married," she pointed out.

"Yes, and as I said before, I can wait and do things right."

"That doesn't mean you can't—"

"Yes, my heart, it does. Do you think I can stop, if I start that? You are too much temptation to me. Go and put on something overwhelmingly ugly—an overcoat. Or a ski suit, if you have one."

"I don't have a ski suit here in summer. I have a black bikini."

"That's worse than nothing! Or better—more tempting and suggestive. Pack it up for the honeymoon."

"Let's go to Cornwall for our honeymoon," she said. "You can start your book."

"On our honeymoon? Much work I'd get done!"

"We'll stay six months, then."

The dinger on the stove informed them the coffee was ready. "I must go," he said, trying to disengage himself.

She pulled him back. "Let it ring," she said, running her fingers through the hair on his neck.

"Tillie, you're trying to *seduce* me!"

"Mmmm," she said, nibbling his ear.

He tightened his grip on her, kissing her ruthlessly, till she was pressing herself against him. He responded for thirty seconds; then pulled himself away and stood up, stretching his neck and straightening his collar around his flushed neck.

"Now see here, young lady, *I* wear the trousers in this family, and they're not unzipped till we're home from the altar. Go and put on your ski suit. I'm pouring us a cup of coffee."

"I bet you make very good coffee, Simon," she said with a sly smile.

"Good to the last drop," he agreed, pulling her up from the sofa.

Silhouette **Romance**

15-Day Free Trial Offer
6 Silhouette Romances

6 Silhouette Romances, free for 15 days! We'll send you 6 new Silhouette Romances to keep for 15 days, absolutely free! If you decide not to keep them, send them back to us. You pay nothing.

Free Home Delivery. But if you enjoy them as much as we think you will, keep them by paying the invoice enclosed with your free trial shipment. We'll pay all shipping and handling charges. You get the convenience of Home Delivery and we pay the postage and handling charge each month.

Don't miss a copy. The Silhouette Book Club is the way to make sure you'll be able to receive every new romance we publish before they're sold out. There is no minimum number of books to buy and you can cancel at any time.

This offer expires March 31, 1984

Silhouette Romance

IT'S YOUR OWN SPECIAL TIME
Contemporary romances for today's women.
Each month, six very special love stories will be yours
from SILHOUETTE. Look for them wherever books are sold
or order now from the coupon below.

$1.50 each

☐ 5 Goforth	☐ 28 Hampson	☐ 54 Beckman	☐ 83 Halston
☐ 6 Stanford	☐ 29 Wildman	☐ 55 LaDame	☐ 84 Vitek
☐ 7 Lewis	☐ 30 Dixon	☐ 56 Trent	☐ 85 John
☐ 8 Beckman	☐ 32 Michaels	☐ 57 John	☐ 86 Adams
☐ 9 Wilson	☐ 33 Vitek	☐ 58 Stanford	☐ 87 Michaels
☐ 10 Caine	☐ 34 John	☐ 59 Vernon	☐ 88 Stanford
☐ 11 Vernon	☐ 35 Stanford	☐ 60 Hill	☐ 89 James
☐ 17 John	☐ 38 Browning	☐ 61 Michaels	☐ 90 Major
☐ 19 Thornton	☐ 39 Sinclair	☐ 62 Halston	☐ 92 McKay
☐ 20 Fulford	☐ 46 Stanford	☐ 63 Brent	☐ 93 Browning
☐ 22 Stephens	☐ 47 Vitek	☐ 71 Ripy	☐ 94 Hampson
☐ 23 Edwards	☐ 48 Wildman	☐ 73 Browning	☐ 95 Wisdom
☐ 24 Healy	☐ 49 Wisdom	☐ 76 Hardy	☐ 96 Beckman
☐ 25 Stanford	☐ 50 Scott	☐ 78 Oliver	☐ 97 Clay
☐ 26 Hastings	☐ 52 Hampson	☐ 81 Roberts	☐ 98 St. George
☐ 27 Hampson	☐ 53 Browning	☐ 82 Dailey	☐ 99 Camp

$1.75 each

☐ 100 Stanford	☐ 114 Michaels	☐ 128 Hampson	☐ 143 Roberts
☐ 101 Hardy	☐ 115 John	☐ 129 Converse	☐ 144 Goforth
☐ 102 Hastings	☐ 116 Lindley	☐ 130 Hardy	☐ 145 Hope
☐ 103 Cork	☐ 117 Scott	☐ 131 Stanford	☐ 146 Michaels
☐ 104 Vitek	☐ 118 Dailey	☐ 132 Wisdom	☐ 147 Hampson
☐ 105 Eden	☐ 119 Hampson	☐ 133 Rowe	☐ 148 Cork
☐ 106 Dailey	☐ 120 Carroll	☐ 134 Charles	☐ 149 Saunders
☐ 107 Bright	☐ 121 Langan	☐ 135 Logan	☐ 150 Major
☐ 108 Hampson	☐ 122 Scofield	☐ 136 Hampson	☐ 151 Hampson
☐ 109 Vernon	☐ 123 Sinclair	☐ 137 Hunter	☐ 152 Halston
☐ 110 Trent	☐ 124 Beckman	☐ 138 Wilson	☐ 153 Dailey
☐ 111 South	☐ 125 Bright	☐ 139 Vitek	☐ 154 Beckman
☐ 112 Stanford	☐ 126 St. George	☐ 140 Erskine	☐ 155 Hampson
☐ 113 Browning	☐ 127 Roberts	☐ 142 Browning	☐ 156 Sawyer

6 brand new Silhouette Special Editions yours for 15 days–Free!

For the reader who wants more…more story…more detail and description…more realism…and more romance…in paperback originals, 1/3 longer than our regular Silhouette Romances. Love lingers longer in new Silhouette Special Editions. Love weaves an intricate, provocative path in a third more pages than you have just enjoyed. It is love as you have always wanted it to be—and more —intriguingly depicted by your favorite Silhouette authors in the inimitable Silhouette style.

15-Day Free Trial Offer

We will send you 6 new Silhouette Special Editions to keep for 15 days absolutely free! If you decide not to keep them, send them back to us, you pay nothing. But if you enjoy them as much as we think you will, keep them and pay the invoice enclosed with your trial shipment. You will then automatically become a member of the Special Edition Book Club and receive 6 more romances every month. There is no minimum number of books to buy and you can cancel at any time.

FREE CHARTER MEMBERSHIP COUPON

**Silhouette Special Editions, Dept. SESB7Q
120 Brighton Road, Clifton, NJ 07012**

Please send me 6 Silhouette Special Editions to keep for 15 days, absolutely free. I understand I am not obligated to join the Silhouette Special Editions Book Club unless I decide to keep them.

Name —————————————————————————

Address ————————————————————————

City —————————————————————————————

State———————————————— Zip ——————————

This offer expires March 31, 1984.

READERS' COMMENTS ON SILHOUETTE ROMANCES:

"I would like to congratulate you on the most wonderful books I've had the pleasure of reading. They are a tremendous joy to those of us who have yet to meet the man of our dreams. From reading your books I quite truly believe that he will some-day appear before me like a prince!"

—L.L.*, Hollandale, MS

"Your books are great, wholesome fiction, always with an upbeat, happy ending. Thank you."

—M.D., Massena, NY

"My boyfriend always teases me about Silhouette Books. He asks me, how's my love life and natu-rally I say terrific, but I tell him that there is always room for a little more romance from Sil-houette."

—F.N., Ontario, Canada

"I would like to sincerely express my gratitude to you and your staff for bringing the pleasure of your publications to my attention. Your books are well written, mature and very contemporary."

—D.D., Staten Island, NY

*names available on request